OFFSIDES

STACY
DRUMTRA-JUBA

Cover, design and typesetting by Mark Juba

Dedicated to all the readers
who have patiently awaited a sequel.
This one's for you!

Chapter One

"Over!" T.J. McKendrick shouted, telling his brother he was open across from him.

Brad sent the puck to him and they tore down the ice on a breakaway. T.J. rocketed a shot to the low corner on the goalie's stick side. The goaltender blocked it with his pads and directed the puck toward a defenseman. Brad swooped in first, catching it on his stick. He flipped it to T.J., yelling, "Around!"

Pulse thundering, T.J. wrapped the puck around the boards. Brad raced there in time to retrieve it. T.J. zoomed in front of the goaltender, ready for the return pass. When his brother snapped the disk back to him, T.J. thrust it into the right side of the cord. Score!

With fifty seconds left in the third period, they now had a four-goal lead. The brothers exchanged fist bumps, each wearing the captain "C" on the left front shoulder of their jerseys.

After an uneventful final minute of play, their teammates mobbed them, spraying up ice chips as they celebrated the season opener shutout.

T.J. and Brad's fourteen-year-old brother Chris skated off the bench. He resembled a slighter version of the team's starters in his helmet with chin straps fastened to his head, dark blue travel jersey with large white numbers on the back and smaller numbers on the sleeves, gloves, padded hockey pants, and blue hockey socks. Unlike the others, no sweat glistened behind his face mask. "Good game. Wish I could've played."

"You're only a freshman," Brad reminded him. "And it's just

the first game."

"Give it time," T.J. agreed, turning to congratulate their goalie, Trey Arenson.

Coach Reynolds stood before them in the locker room, short and stocky with a bald head and drooping walrus mustache. No matter how much he skated with the team, he never lost his pouch of a stomach. "You deserved that win tonight. You boys gave a great effort. We can make it all the way this year, and this team just took the first step. I want to see that same intensity and focus at practice next week."

After the boys had showered and were leaving the building, T.J.'s cell signaled an incoming text. His heart rate picked up when he saw the sender's name. The assistant hockey coach at Boston College. He'd Cc'd a note to Brad and T.J.

I was in the area and came by for the first two periods. Good job. I couldn't stay for the whole game, but wanted to wish you both luck this season. Stay in touch.

T.J. exchanged a grin with his brother, who was walking a few feet ahead of him. BC was a perennial hockey juggernaut and T.J.'s first choice college. The hockey staff had seemed interested in them junior year, and this showed they were still on the watch list.

On the bus ride home, Brad and T.J. shared a seat in back. Snow flurries dusted the air outside, flakes wetting the dark window. He and Brad were fraternal twins. While no one would mistake them for identical, they looked related with their athletic builds and longish blond hair that spilled out the back of their helmets. T.J. spent more time on his, combing fingers through it when the locks were semi-dry, guiding it to the side, and coaxing a tendril across his forehead. Brad just swept his hair off his face and let it flow in tousled waves. They both worked hard on their physiques, following an ambitious weightlifting regimen.

Since strength and conditioning was part of the NCAA Division I hockey training program, college players often gained at least twenty pounds of lean muscle mass. Most high-level players spent a couple years in a junior league before college, some through age twenty, which meant that many D1 hockey players were twenty-five in their last season. To compete with older, bigger guys, the twins had expanded their training routine.

T.J. glanced at his brother, who was scrolling through text messages. During a rocky period where they'd drifted apart, T.J. was forced to leave his private school last year and join Brad at Bayview High. Once they adjusted to the unwelcome change, they'd pursued their goals—both on the ice and off—together.

He and Brad had emailed Hockey East conference coaches and junior league scouts and were now in semi-regular contact. They'd visited campuses together, touring the facilities, watching practices and games, and meeting players and staff. Although they hadn't pitched themselves as a package deal, they were talking to the same people.

For a high school star, college hockey coaches sometimes extended a verbal promise to reserve an athletic scholarship, unofficially saving a spot on the future roster. They still expected the player to develop in junior and wouldn't formalize the offer until down the line. Usually though, scouts approached seasoned junior league standouts. T.J. hoped he defeated the odds and received a commitment out of high school. When he used to watch the Frozen Four—the semifinals and final game of the NCAA Men's Ice Hockey Championship—on TV as a kid, he never imagined how tough it would be to reach that elite level. For some players, the dream never worked out, and they had to set their sights on Division III.

"So . . . what school are you hoping for?" T.J. asked.

Brad slid his phone into the pocket of his letterman jacket. "BC and BU are my top choices, then Providence and Merrimack. I'm hoping for BC the most since I've always been an Eagles fan. How about you?"

"Same. They're all great, but I really liked the staff at BC and the facilities."

If Boston College didn't offer them both a commitment though, T.J. would rather go where they could play together. They had great chemistry as linemates with every rush up the ice. Brad was fast, strong on the boards, won battles in the corners, and possessed solid forechecking skills. He had that magical ability to score and create plays for his teammates, making him the type of winger that coaches sought. Their friends called it twin telepathy the way they killed penalties together and always knew where the other would be.

Yet they also had a long history of competition. At practice, the atmosphere occasionally grew heated. That was T.J.'s only concern, whether their sibling rivalry would flare up.

As usual, Brad seemed to read his mind. "Do you think we should try to go to college together? Or play against each other? Either way, there's bound to be violence."

T.J. saw the hopeful expression on Brad's face and grinned. "I wouldn't mind having some twin telepathy."

"Might come in handy," Brad said. "Especially for you."

"Any chance you can leave your ego behind?"

"Nope. Yours would be too lonely. So are we going for it?"

"Yeah. Let's do it."

It relieved T.J. to have one decision made. Not that getting recruited as a pair was guaranteed, but now they knew how to handle offers.

They were lucky to grow up in Massachusetts, which like Minnesota, New York, and Michigan, was a hockey factory that produced quality players. Since New England boasted powerhouse college teams, and the coaches scouted in their own geographic area, it was also easier to attract attention here. As for junior hockey, the United States Hockey League, the largest supplier of NCAA hockey talent, was headquartered in Chicago and centered in the Midwest. T.J. and Brad hoped to get drafted into the USHL league.

When had life gotten so complicated? T.J. popped in his earbuds and leaned against his seat, listening to his favorite band, ready to zone out.

Twenty minutes later, the bus pulled into the school parking lot where their girlfriends awaited them. Brad climbed down the steps and locked Sherry in a kiss, brushing back her blonde side braid. They'd been together for a year, unlike T.J. and Kayla, who had dated seven weeks. That was a record for T.J. Until now, he'd never dated a girl longer than a month. By then, they always got too needy. He preferred to keep things casual, since after graduation he could wind up in a state like Iowa or Illinois, playing a rigorous sixty-game schedule not counting exhibition and playoff games. He didn't envy Brad maintaining a long-distance relationship.

"Who wants pizza?" Their teammate Trey, six-foot-two with 200 pounds of hard muscle, ran a finger through his rumpled black mullet. He'd broken up with his girlfriend over the summer, but that didn't prevent him from tagging along on his friends' dates.

"I'm in, but we've got to drive Chris home first," T.J. said.

It still seemed weird that his kid brother was in high school. Freshmen boys looked like middle-schoolers to T.J.

"Come on," Chris protested.

"You've got an earlier curfew than we do."

"Mom would let me go. It's just out to eat."

"It's okay with me if Little M hangs out with us," Trey interjected, using his nickname for Chris.

"Call home and make sure it's cool," Brad said.

Chris yanked out his cell phone and turned away. Their mother gave permission, and soon they sat in a long booth at Misty's Pizza Palace, a popular restaurant with red and white checkered tables and wood-fired ovens.

Beside T.J., Kayla sipped her strawberry lemonade. She played softball and field hockey and was pursuing athletic scholarships herself. Kayla had attracted him because of her cute freckled face, glossy red mane, and impressive sports stats, but her laid-back personality might make her the perfect girlfriend for his senior year. Unlike other girls he'd dated, she gave him space. If he didn't have a chance to text or call, Kayla never acted insecure. She wasn't the type to blow up his phone with messages or to complain that he spent more time on the ice than with her.

"Sherry, have you applied to colleges yet?" Kayla asked.

"I'm hoping to get into Florida State," Sherry replied from across the table. "I'm working on the essay. The best and hardest parts of being a teenager."

Florida State? That was news to T.J. though it made sense. Sherry grew up in Tallahassee, moving to Bayview last year after her father's job transfer. She must miss the warm climate and her old friends. He wondered how Brad felt about her going to Florida. T.J. noted the tight set of Brad's jaw and guessed he wasn't happy.

"Essays are tough," Kayla said. "Good luck with it. You're from Florida, right?"

Sherry nodded. "I want to room with my best friend from back home. Cross your fingers we both get in."

"I will."

"Trey, any news from scouts?" Brad asked abruptly, gazing past Sherry to his friend on the inside of the booth.

"I'm getting some interest from the Jersey Hitmen," Trey said. "Their starting goalie is going to the University of Vermont next fall. I sent the assistant coach our schedule last night."

Trey wanted to play for the NCDC, a junior league in the Northeast. Chris immersed himself in his Instagram feed as Trey answered a question from Kayla. All this senior talk must bore him. Before T.J. could draw his younger brother into the conversation, their teammate Glen McCann swaggered over, casting his usual scowl. He had an unsightly mop of dark hair that streamed past his shoulders, dark stubble peppering his upper lip and chin, and a perpetual dark expression.

"Well, if it isn't the famous McKendrick twins. And Arenson, what a surprise. Don't you have any friends besides these losers?"

"Get a life, McCann," Brad said.

"Showing off as usual tonight, huh, McKendrick?"

"Maybe Reynolds would play you more if your passes didn't keep getting intercepted." Brad folded his arms across his chest.

"You think you're so great, don't you?" scoffed McCann. "Let's see how you do after high school when you're in a bigger pond. I bet you choke."

"I've already played in a bigger pond, and didn't see you at the camps where I worked with coaches from the Colorado Avalanche and Carolina Hurricanes. Oh, that's right. You weren't invited."

T.J. detected the fire in his brother's eyes. Brad, the hotheaded twin, was thirty seconds away from punching McCann in the face and getting them kicked out of the restaurant. "Come on, guys, knock it off. You're on the same team."

Just then, the waitress approached with their pizzas. McCann stalked toward his friends seated near the far wall. The waitress lowered her trays onto the table and regarded the group with a furrowed brow. "Everything okay over here?"

"Everything's fine," Kayla assured her. "Thank you."

Once the waitress left, Sherry touched Brad's shoulder. "Why do you let him get to you? Just ignore him."

"I'm not ignoring some asshole mouthing off," Brad snapped.

Uh-oh. T.J. didn't miss the hurt that flickered across her face. While Brad had a temper, he rarely lost it with Sherry.

Blinking, she angled herself away from him. "Fine. Then let McCann win. You're giving him what he wants. A reaction."

"I'm getting some pizza before Trey eats it all," T.J. interrupted. "Kayla, do you want cheese or pepperoni?"

"Pepperoni," she answered quickly. "How about you, Chris?"

They ate in peace though Sherry and Brad didn't say much. When the boys arrived home an hour later, their mother was lying on the couch, her hand covering her forehead. A few weeks earlier, she'd left her part-time hospital job and started a full-time position as a home care nurse. T.J. didn't know how she balanced her patients and her four sons' hockey schedules, appointments, carpools, school events, and hockey booster meetings. T.J. tried to help, but he was busy, too.

"Hey, Mom," he said.

She sat up and managed a strained smile. "Hi, guys."

"You look tired."

"Jory had a long practice tonight. Congratulations. I heard you won."

Brad filled her in on the BC scout, and her smile broadened.

"Sounds like a good game for him to see. Wish I could've been there, especially for Chris's debut as a Bayview Jet."

"You didn't miss anything," Chris said with a shrug. "I didn't even play."

"You were still in a varsity uniform. It's hard when you boys have hockey at the same time. Which seems to be always."

Despite the juggling and her frequent complaints about 6:30 a.m. practices, their mother loved the sport. Over the years, she had spent countless hours bundled in a fleece sweatshirt, turtleneck, wool socks, and fur-lined boots, watching her boys play. Wrapped in a blanket, she would drink coffee and chat with the other moms. She had grown up in rinks as a competitive skater, and her older brothers played hockey. Their mother taught T.J. and Brad to skate when they were eighteen months old. Skating felt as natural to T.J. as walking.

"It's okay," Brad said. "It's not like you can clone yourself."

"Wouldn't that be nice?" she mused. "I'll get to as many games as I can. Not only is this Chris's first season, it's the last for you and T.J."

"I'm going to bed," Chris grumbled, elbowing past T.J. to the stairs.

Maybe it bothered him more than he was saying that neither parent made it to the game. Lately, their father worked long hours keeping his architectural firm afloat and was less available during the week. Between their swamped, separated parents and his banishment to the sidelines, Chris had seemed off all night.

While his twin went in search of food, T.J. knocked on Chris's door and entered disaster central. Plates with crusted residue, a half-dozen used glasses, an apple core, and a banana peel littered his nightstand, and dirty clothes overflowed from his hamper. Miscellaneous Lego pieces, Pokémon cards, cords, and comic books made the floor an obstacle course.

T.J. almost told his brother to put the plates and glasses in the dishwasher and do his laundry tomorrow, but now wasn't the time to nag Chris about his chores, not when he seemed so glum. "Hey."

"What do you want?" Chris asked, sprawled on his unmade bed. Behind him hung a wall decal of the Boston Bruins logo.

"You know you'll get more shifts next year, right? Once the seniors graduate, the coaches will be counting on you to help rebuild the team."

"I'm just as good as Matt is," Chris said, referring to his brothers' linemate. "He's always screwing around at practice, but they're gonna keep playing him in front of me while I'm freezing on the bench."

T.J. sighed. Like all the McKendrick boys, Chris lived and breathed hockey. Bobbleheads of NHL players and autographed pucks cluttered his bureau. When he wasn't on the ice or using one of their shooting pads, he was challenging his siblings and friends to street hockey or air hockey. But nothing compared to an actual game before a cheering crowd.

"The coaches talked to you about playing JV and starting, or playing varsity and possibly seeing a few shifts on the third or fourth line," T.J. said. "You wanted varsity, so you've got to pay your dues. It's an accomplishment just to make the team."

Last year, the Jets were selected for the Super Eight tournament, which featured the top ten public and private high school teams in Massachusetts. They lost in the finals at the TD Garden, a heart-wrenching loss.

"I won't feel like part of it if I don't play."

"You have an important job. To push the starters at practice and make us work for the puck. By doing that, you'll get better and better and will see some shifts. Trust me. We've all been there."

"I guess." Chris didn't sound convinced.

"I'll try to give you some tips at practice."

As T.J. left and closed the door, his ten-year-old brother Jory stepped out into the hallway in his pajamas—an old hockey jersey and sweatpants. "Hey, Jor, what're you doing awake?"

"I can't fall asleep." Jory hesitated. "Do you think Dad will come in the house when he picks us up tomorrow?"

T.J. doubted it. Their parents were seeing a marriage counselor, but it wasn't helping, considering how much they avoided each other. "I don't know."

"When is he moving back in?"

Probably never. But T.J. didn't voice his suspicion out loud. "You've got to face that he might not. Whatever happens though, you'll still see him a lot, just like you do now."

"It's not the same," Jory murmured, hanging his head, his wavy blond hair mussed from his pillow. "And his place is boring. All my stuff is here."

T.J. wished he felt the way Jory did. Instead, he was the worst son ever as his father's absence gave him a break from Dad's harping. He didn't want his parents to split up for good though. T.J. wondered how much of the rift between them was his fault. Mom supported his NHL dream while Dad thought he should be a lawyer or a doctor since his grades were high enough to compete for valedictorian. He had overheard arguments with Mom insisting his father pressured T.J. too much, and Dad claiming she was too lenient.

"You're right, it's tough," T.J. acknowledged over the lump in his throat. "But staying up all night worrying won't help."

Jory released a heavy sigh. "Want to hang out for a little while?"

After the tiring game, T.J. would rather go to bed, but he couldn't refuse his forlorn kid brother.

"Sure." Clapping a hand on Jory's shoulder, T.J. followed him into his dark room.

Chapter Two

The next night, Brad and T.J. watched the Bruins game in their father's living room, so different from the one at home, the gray and beige accents bland and the couch hard. It opened into a double bed, which their younger brothers shared on weekends while the twins got the bunks in the guest room. The more furniture their father purchased, the more Brad suspected he wasn't coming home.

Their dad's condo was on the building's second floor. The Crestwood Manor complex had a small fitness center and a playground, however the cramped living quarters frustrated the boys. Brad wasn't a neat freak like T.J., but even he got irked by the backpacks, duffel bags, school books, mounds of dirty clothes, and hockey sticks crammed into the corners. To make the place more appealing, their father stocked up on junk food and bought an Xbox for the guest room, which Chris and Jory were playing right now.

His father, Thomas McKendrick Sr., strode into the room and frowned at the TV. It wasn't a secret that he'd rather watch anything besides hockey. Dad sank into the recliner. "Thomas, I logged into the parent portal," he told T.J. "If you want to be valedictorian, you'd better bring up that AP Statistics grade."

"I'm trying," T.J. said.

"A ninety-four average isn't enough to get out of the number three slot," Dad reminded him.

"I told you, I'm trying."

"Have you been working on college applications?"

"Dad, we've been through this. I'm playing junior next year."

Their father lifted the remote control from the coffee table and lowered the TV volume. Brad exchanged an exasperated glance with T.J. He'd wanted to relax in front of the Bruins game, but the tension between his father and brother was thickening every second.

"Not that again. How can you put hockey before your education?"

Brad knew their father was speaking to T.J. Despite them sharing the same goals, Dad only gave one of them a hard time. Brad used to resent how Dad expected great things from T.J. and not from him. While it still stung that his father barely noticed his Bs and occasional A, Brad didn't envy the pressure on his twin. Though a little recognition for his accomplishments beyond hockey would be nice.

"Dad, we're talking to colleges all the time," T.J. said, his green eyes narrowing beneath his Bruins cap. "The whole point of playing junior is to get an athletic scholarship. Ninety-five percent of USHL players get a Division I offer. And over 90 percent of college hockey players graduate. That's one of the highest rates in college sports."

"Thomas, your grades are strong enough to earn academic scholarships now, so why delay your education? And if you got accepted into an Ivy League school, they don't offer scholarships, but we should meet the requirements for financial aid."

"Dad, T.J. can apply for academic scholarships after we graduate, not just senior year," Brad said. "Besides, even if Harvard accepted him tomorrow, the coaches would want him to play junior. It's rare to go from high school to D1. Most eighteen-year-old freshmen come from junior, not high school."

He and T.J. had memorized the facts before telling their parents they intended to postpone college. They explained that the USHL was tuition-free, providing coaching, training, and development at no charge. The league also paid for equipment, housing, and travel expenses. It relieved their mother that junior players lived with a billet family, a local host family screened and interviewed by the league, rather than on their own. Since sixteen-year-olds were eligible for junior, she appreciated their desire to graduate from Bayview rather than finish high school elsewhere. Dad seemed okay with the junior route for Brad, but not for T.J.

"I'm not saying he has to give up hockey," their father said. "He can take an academic scholarship and still play on an intramural team."

"Thanks for your support, Dad." T.J. grabbed his sneakers from the closet and strode out of the condo. The door rattled behind him.

Brad glanced at his father, who never understood his sons' obsession with hockey. He'd encouraged golf and tennis, but all four boys had ice in their blood. During hockey practices, Dad went straight to the room that overlooked the rink, sitting at the table and working on his laptop. Sometimes he even stayed there for games.

"Dad, I really think we have a chance at the NHL," Brad said. "Going to the National Player Development Camp in New York was a big deal. We beat out a lot of good players to get there and worked with some NHL coaches."

Not to mention the other honors he and T.J. had accumulated like All Star status, MVP awards, inclusion on the Boston newspapers' dream teams, and invitations to elite showcases and festivals. Brad hoped his efforts led to a successful pro career. If it didn't pan out, he'd still have a bachelor's degree in communications with concentrations in broadcasting and journalism, but Brad would do whatever was necessary to achieve his goal.

"Brad, having a successful career in the NHL is a longshot," Dad said. "Sure, you guys might play in a few games or even a season or two, but the odds are you'd spend most of your career bouncing around the minors. Do you know most minor league athletes take side jobs during the off-season?"

"AHL salaries are decent. It's not like Single-A minor league baseball." Based in the U.S. and Canada, the American Hockey League was the primary developmental league for the NHL. Brad followed the Providence Bruins, AHL affiliate of the Boston Bruins. "But give us some credit. We'll know when to quit."

Dad sighed. "Let's save this argument for another time. You already know I support your path to college. Your talent opens doors that might otherwise be closed, and an athletic scholarship would help us financially. But your brother doesn't need hockey. He's always been at the top of the class and can get into any school he wants. Playing junior isn't a justifiable reason for him to put off his education. He's not in the same situation as you."

Brad focused his attention on the Bruins game. He had improved his grades last year, seeking tutoring from T.J. and Sherry, making sure his academic performance met the NCAA eligibility requirements. He'd taken video production classes, covered sports articles for the school newspaper, and even developed his interest in writing stories by scouring the websites of the Horror Writers Association and the Science Fiction and Fantasy Writers of America.

But his father only viewed him as a jock. Brad hadn't told his parents about his fiction as sharing his writing made him self-conscious. Their father criticized T.J. for being third in the class; if that didn't impress him, there was no way Brad's mostly unfinished stories would wow him.

"Dad, we'll never agree on this," he muttered. "Sometimes you have to follow your dreams and see what happens."

"What if he doesn't get an athletic scholarship?" his father countered. "What will college admissions offices think of him goofing off for two years?"

Brad set his jaw. "Dad, it's not goofing off. We'll have a tough schedule with the conditioning, practices, and games. The teams do community service too. Some guys take a couple college classes and get a part-time job. That's one reason so many hockey players earn their degree. They learn time management."

"T.J. already knows how to manage his time," his father said, raising the television volume and ending the conversation.

That night, Brad lay awake in the top bunk, staring at the ceiling. A night light glimmered in the corner and shadows bathed the small television, TV stand, and student desk. All the discussion about junior and college reminded him how drastically his life was changing. His parents splitting up last December with no reconciliation in sight. Playing his final season of high school hockey with friends he'd known for years. And even though Brad believed he had a chance of making the NHL, the long winding road ahead scared the hell out of him.

What if he didn't like his host family? Even though they got on his nerves, Brad would miss his own boisterous family. What if he didn't click with his new coaches or had a difficult time adjusting to a higher level of play? Then there was Sherry. His friends thought their relationship was a high school thing. Brad thought it was more. If he joined a junior team in the Northeast rather than the Midwest, could he talk her out of Florida?

In the bottom bunk, T.J. shifted, and the mattress creaked. "You awake?"

"Yeah," Brad said.

"Thanks for trying with Dad. I'm so sick of him pushing me about college. It's probably better I'm not going next fall. I'd have no clue what to major in."

"What happened to management and leadership?"

"That's just what I've been telling scouts. You're lucky to have your major picked out."

Having an interest in broadcasting didn't mean Brad would excel at it. As their father stated, academics wasn't his strength, and college was harder than high school. Brad sighed, his stomach clenching in a knot.

"What's wrong?" T.J. asked.

It was quiet except for a car driving into the resident parking lot. Brad didn't know how much to admit. What was he supposed to say? That he feared getting homesick and not fitting in? That despite his big talk, he worried that he wouldn't be good enough?

"Is it Sherry and the Florida thing?"

"Yeah. It's Sherry." Might as well confess that much since T.J. suspected it was bothering him. "I'm wondering whether she'd stay if I played junior locally."

"You mean in the NCDC?"

The National Collegiate Development Conference was a tuition-free junior league in the Northeast, making it an attractive opportunity for players throughout the region. Brad rolled onto his side and peered over the edge of his bed though he couldn't see T.J.'s face in the darkness.

"It's a good league. A lot of their guys are getting commitments. Trey wants to get on one of those teams."

"Yeah, but I thought we were both going for the USHL," T.J. said.

They'd selected the more established USHL as a first choice because so many D1 players and NHL draft picks had ties to the league. Brad and T.J. met some scouts at camp and had been corresponding with several over email. They might not get on the same team, but they'd agreed this was their ideal steppingstone.

"What, I can't change my mind?" Brad leaned up on his elbow, glaring down at the lower bunk.

"Because of a girl?" T.J. asked sharply. "You're seventeen."

"Sherry's not just some girl. You have a new girlfriend every other week, so don't go giving me relationship advice." Brad and Sherry disagreed over how long it would take his brother to dump Kayla. Sherry expected them to attend Prom together. Brad gave it till mid-January before T.J. claimed she was too clingy and moved on to someone else.

Swearing under his breath, T.J. got up and crossed the room. He switched on the light, and Brad winced. "Damn it, T.J."

T.J. paced in his Bayview T-shirt and sweatpants. They both wore exercise clothes to bed and worked out when they woke up. "Even if you two stayed in New England, how often do you think you'd see her? Your life will revolve around hockey. You'll have games on weekends, a lot of them away games. She'll be busy with school. I don't get the logic here."

"I'd see her a lot more than if she's in Florida and I'm in freakin' Nebraska," Brad growled.

"All I'm saying is you'll be wrapped up in the team. Do you really think it's fair to pressure her to give up Florida? I get that you'll miss her. But you'll both come home sometimes. In between, you can FaceTime and text."

Brad flopped onto his back, the fight seeping out of him. "You think I'm being selfish?"

"You're just not thinking this through."

"But long-distance is hard. It might not work."

"Dude, it's your high school girlfriend. Stop stressing over this. Who knows if you'll even be together next year?" T.J. flicked off the light.

***

Sunday evening after Jory's hockey game, their father drove the boys home. He parked in the driveway of their gray Colonial-style house with its steep pointed roof, but didn't turn off the ignition. Their mother had decorated while they were gone, mounting a giant candy cane on the front door, sticking snowflake decals to the windows, and adorning the mailbox with a plaid scarf and a pair of old skates.

"Can't you come in?" Jory, wedged in back between Brad and Chris, unbuckled his seatbelt.

"Not today, Jory," their father replied.

"Today?" Chris snorted. "You never come inside anymore. How will you get back together if you never see each other?" He opened the door and slammed it behind him.

Sighing, their father grasped the steering wheel, and Brad almost sympathized with him. Almost. His parents were both acting childish.

"Bye, Dad." His head bowed, Jory followed Chris out, fetched his sticks and gear from the trunk, and shuffled toward the front steps.

"You're not getting back together, are you?" Brad asked.

His father hesitated and switched off the engine. "No," he said, and the air rushed from Brad's lungs. "We're getting a divorce."

"When were you going to tell us?" T.J. asked bitterly from the passenger seat. "When the papers were signed?"

"We just made the decision. Your mother wanted to wait until after the holidays."

The holidays? What a joke. Brad's fists curled inside the pockets of his blue and white varsity jacket. For the first time, Dad hadn't attended Thanksgiving dinner with Brad's grandparents, aunts, uncles, and cousins on his mother's side. Instead, the boys had leftovers with their father, other grandmother, and a great-aunt on Black Friday. Christmas loomed in two weeks with New Year's on its heels, signaling the last five months of high school. All that excited Brad about the holidays was the Christmas tournament scheduled during break. The Bayview Jets were defending champions with T.J. and Brad finally joining forces last year after a turbulent start as teammates.

"You didn't even try to make it work," Brad said.

"We did try," Dad responded. "We grew in different directions. That happens sometimes even if we don't want it to. Your mom is a great mother, but we don't get along well as a couple. I'll always be here for you though. Nothing will ever change that."

Brad and T.J. sat in silence, digesting the news. It wasn't a surprise, yet that didn't make it any easier to hear.

"Do me a favor and don't mention this to your brothers. I'll talk to your mother and see if she still wants to wait."

After their father's car disappeared around the corner, the twins lingered in the dim driveway. A wintry chill pervaded the air. Brad spoke first. "Well, that sucks."

"Yeah," T.J. muttered.

They entered the house and dropped their bags onto the floor. Their mother glanced up from the armchair where she was on her laptop, filling out paperwork for her job. Lights blinked on the artificial Christmas tree, flickering beneath the gold garland and reflecting onto the shiny bulbs.

Brad spotted his hand reindeer from kindergarten and his painted snowman from second grade dangling on the branches. He'd never minded an artificial tree before, but this year it looked phony. So did the stockings hanging from the fireplace with all their names except Dad's spelled in green glitter. His mother had wrapped a dozen presents so far and spritzed forest pine scent mist in the air, but it wouldn't be a real Christmas just like the fake tree wouldn't transform into a real one.

"Did you have a good time?" Mom asked.

"Dad told us," Brad said after making sure his younger brothers weren't in earshot.

She sat up straighter. "About what?"

"What do you think?"

"I can't believe he did that. We were going to tell you together. That's just like him to . . ." She broke off, catching herself. Brad watched her moisten her lips and fumble for words. Their counselor must have advised them not to badmouth each other around the kids.

"We asked him point blank," T.J. interrupted. "Chris and Jory weren't there."

"I suppose that put him in a difficult situation. I'm sorry, you caught me off guard." She tucked back a wisp of her long blonde hair. "I know this must be disappointing. But we always fought. About everything."

Brad nodded, grudgingly.

"Things will stay the way they are," Mom said. "Your dad will continue taking Chris and Jory on weekends and some school vacations. You're getting older and have your own plans, but you can join them as much as you want. And if you ever just need a break and some quiet, I'm sure Dad would love to have you anytime."

She paused. "Are you two okay about this?"

"I guess we've been expecting it," T.J. answered. "What about you? Are you okay?"

"I'm getting there," she said, but Brad wasn't so sure.

A half hour later, Brad stood at the end of the driveway and fired a puck off the long shooting pad. He and his brothers sprayed it with Pledge to keep the surface slippery; the pad was much better for their stick blades than the rough pavement.

Brad aimed a series of wrist shots at the wide net he'd positioned before the garage. Thanks to him and his brothers, scratches scarred the white double doors. Chris and Jory would wear roller blades and arrange trash barrels inside the net, creating a makeshift goaltender, angling shots around the bins or banking them off the goal post. Their father used to complain about them moving the barrels. Not anymore.

T.J. came out the front door in his Bayview High jacket and jogged down the steps carrying his stick. Brad hadn't bothered with a coat, too distracted to notice the cold. His sneakered feet had felt unsteady until he fell into the familiar calming rhythm of blade connecting with puck.

"Can I take some shots?" T.J. asked.

Brad stepped aside and his brother drove a few pucks into the net.

"Can you imagine if one of them ever remarries?" T.J. said.

Brad had hoped to get in "the zone" where the world faded away, but T.J.'s arrival jolted him back to reality. "That would be weird."

He couldn't picture his parents dating anyone else though he'd never envisioned them divorcing either. His mom and dad had never acted as close as Sherry's parents, who held hands and embarrassed her with their PDA, however, the frequent arguments just started a couple years ago.

Brad gathered the pucks, ready to throw himself into another round of shooting, determined to quiet his racing mind.

***

Brad knew T.J. was right about Sherry and her college plans. If she wanted to attend school in Florida, he should support her. Regardless of where he played, his schedule would be insane. But as he lay on Sherry's couch watching a movie with her nestled in his arms, his common sense evaporated.

"If I were on a junior team in the Northeast, maybe even Massachusetts, would you consider a school here?" Brad asked.

She sat up, swinging her legs off his and gnawing her bottom lip. "Brad . . . I love that you want to be near me. But won't you be traveling a lot on the weekends?"

He nodded and let her continue listing all the reasons this was a bad idea.

"I'll be busy with classes during the week and you'll have practice," she went on. "When you were doing the split season, practically the only time we saw each other was in school."

He and T.J. had played in a travel league between August and November. It would resume after the high school season ended, allowing members to play for their schools in the interim. In the past, their mother vetoed a split season, wanting them to participate in other activities besides hockey. Even though she was a devoted hockey mom, she wasn't like the obsessed parents who hired strength coaches for their twelve-year-olds and blasted daily social media updates about her kids' stats. But Mom understood that the game was getting serious. And so did his girlfriend.

"What if I stayed and you got traded?" Sherry asked. "You can get traded in junior, right?"

Brad sighed and leaned his head against the armrest. "Yeah. It can happen."

"You don't even know where you'll be next year. Once my acceptances come in, I can't keep waiting. And just because you prefer certain teams or leagues doesn't mean you'll wind up there, right?"

"Forget it, it was a stupid idea." His gaze lingered on their junior prom picture atop the mantel, him in his black tux and Sherry stunning in her beaded turquoise dress.

Guys would pursue her in college, no question. As a hockey player, it wouldn't be hard for him to meet girls, either. Once he and Sherry went in separate directions, it would be much easier to date other people.

"I've just been thinking about how everything will be different next year," he admitted.

Sober, Sherry reached over and squeezed his hand. "That's been bothering me too. My mom told me if it's meant to be, it will be. I have to believe that's true." Her pink-polished fingernails dug into his palm. "You'll try the long-distance thing, won't you? We'll see how it goes?"

She'd cared enough to discuss it with her mother, so that had to be a good sign, right? Still, once Sherry was in college, he knew her mom would encourage her to date other guys rather than pine after a hockey player boyfriend. Her parents liked him, but he and Sherry were only seventeen.

His love life was doomed, anyway. His parents' marriage had failed. They'd been his role models, so what chance did he have for a successful long-term relationship with Sherry or anyone else?

"Yeah. Of course." Brad pulled himself upright and drew her closer to him.

As they kissed, he tried to suppress the disturbing thoughts crowding his mind. Their uncertain future. His parents divorcing—a revelation he hadn't told Sherry yet as she would probe into his feelings, and Brad wasn't in the mood to discuss it. Then there was adjusting to a new team, a new state, and a new family. And during breaks, returning home to his real family that would never be the same again.

Chapter Three

Thursday afternoon, while they waited for their Graphic Design class to begin, Trey remarked from the desk beside T.J.'s, "You won't believe who I saw Little M hanging out with today."

"Who?" T.J. flipped through his notebook for his homework assignment. Chris was probably interested in a girl. He "dated" a couple in middle school, which meant they talked in the hallway and texted each other for a few weeks.

"*McCann.*" Trey's tone reflected his disbelief.

T.J.'s inner radar shot up. "They couldn't have been hanging out. McCann must've been bothering him."

"I don't think so. They were talking in front of Chris's locker. Didn't look like they were arguing."

T.J. rubbed the back of his neck. The only talking McCann ever did with a McKendrick was trash talk.

When T.J. transferred to Bayview, McCann considered him a threat as they both played center. McCann and Brad had never gotten along either, and since last Friday's run-in, they'd been checking each other hard during practice. McCann cooperated during games as he wanted to win and build his own stats, but played for himself, not the team. He hung out with troublemakers who didn't play hockey, and his one friend on the Bayview Jets moved over the summer.

"He must be using Chris to rattle you and Brad," Trey said.

"But what's Chris's excuse?" T.J. asked.

At practice that day, Coach Reynolds and his slight bespectacled assistant Coach Ryan drilled the JV and varsity teams at stations for continuous passing and shooting, stickhandling, and figure-eight passing and shooting. When Chris skated to the bench for a water break, T.J. followed him. He'd mention McCann later, in private, but for now he had some hockey pointers.

"You've been doing great, but I noticed something with your stickhandling," T.J. said. "You're gripping your stick too tight with your bottom hand. Your hand goes up and down instead of side to side. Loosen up that grip and control the puck with your top hand. Keep your head up more too, so you're more aware of what's going on around you."

"What are you talking about?" Chris demanded, lifting his chin a notch. "I know all that already. My stickhandling is fine."

TJ. had expected gratitude, not attitude. "If you want to get off the bench, you need to take constructive criticism."

Chris slammed down his water bottle. "You can't tell me what to do. You're not the coach."

"I'm a captain, and you're the freshman who griped about sitting out the first game," T.J. shot back, irritation lancing through him.

"I don't need your help." Chris vaulted over the boards and skated back onto the ice.

What had happened to the kid brother who idolized him? T.J. rejoined the figure-eight passing and shooting drill and waited with Brad for their turns.

"What was that with Chris?" Brad asked.

"I gave him some tips, and he got pissed off."

"What for?"

"How should I know?"

Brad swung around to watch their brother working the puck at the stickhandling station. Chris was drilling with Greg, a sophomore forward who'd played last season. "Seems like he's doing okay now."

Chris had improved his grip, T.J. observed. Even if he was too stubborn to admit his mistakes, at least he heeded the advice.

In the locker room after practice, T.J. slid his empty water bottle into his equipment bag alongside the extra laces, tape rolls, stick wax, and other paraphernalia. He spotted Chris and McCann by the door, zipped his gear bag over his shoulder, and approached them.

"Chris, come on," T.J. said shortly. "We've got to go."

"In a minute," Chris replied, leaning against the large bulletin board that featured practice and game schedules, a flyer for the upcoming Christmas tournament, and the rosters for JV and varsity.

"Come on," T.J. repeated.

He wished Brad hadn't left the locker room although with his twin's temper and history with McCann that might have triggered a fight outside the coach's office. Reynolds could be your biggest advocate, calling scouts on his own time and inviting them to games, but none of the players enjoyed seeing him angry.

"You don't have to follow his orders," McCann cut in. "I can give you a ride."

"Did I ask for your opinion? Chris, let's go. Now."

Chris glanced from one to the other and then mumbled to McCann, "See you later." He thrust open the door that led to the corridor.

The brothers didn't speak on the way through the arena, passing the training room, snack bar, pro shop and skate sharpening service, skate rental area, and ticket desk. The Bayview School Department operated the rink and had it renovated a few years ago, charging figure skating programs, Jory's youth hockey league, and men's leagues to reserve the ice. T.J. and Kayla skated here a couple weeks ago during the public hours. It had become a second home to him—definitely a more welcome one than his father's condo.

When they reached T.J.'s car, Brad was sitting in the passenger seat and Trey in back. T.J. started the engine and the heater, and turned to Chris, who had joined Trey in the backseat. "Since when are you pals with McCann?"

Chris shrugged and tapped out a message on his phone. "I don't know."

"Wait a minute." Frostiness edged Brad's voice colder than the 38-degree temperature outside. He swiveled around toward his younger brother. "Are you kidding me? You're friends with McCann?"

"So what? I can be friends with who I want."

Trey groaned and covered his face with his hands. "Little M, you're killing me here. Out of all the guys on JV and varsity, you pick him as a buddy? Why can't you hang out with someone like Greg? He's a nice kid."

Ignoring him, Chris glared at his brothers. "You guys are the co-captains. Shouldn't you want everyone to get along?"

"McCann doesn't know the meaning of getting along," Brad said. "He's using you to get to T.J. and me."

"Don't flatter yourself," Chris retorted. "Everything isn't always about you two."

T.J. shrugged as Brad looked at him in bewilderment. Chris was a pain sometimes, like most siblings were, but he'd always wanted to be just like them. This rebelliousness didn't fit the kid brother who had followed them around for years.

"Hey, guys," Trey broke in. "Not to interrupt or anything, but people are starving back here. My mom's cooking steak tonight. Can we debate this later?"

"Fine," Brad said, facing front. "But this isn't over."

"It is for me." Chris returned his attention to his cell phone.

Irritated, T.J. flicked on the radio and shifted the car into drive. They dropped off Trey a few blocks from school and headed home.

When their house came into view, T.J saw their father's Cadillac in the driveway, blocking his entrance to the garage. He parked beside the Cadillac and traded an uneasy glance with

Brad. Something was definitely up. Were their parents telling Chris and Jory about the divorce tonight? If so, with Chris's mood, they had picked a lousy time.

"Dad's here. Maybe he's staying for dinner." Chris climbed out of the backseat and sprinted toward the front door, not bothering to retrieve his hockey gear.

"I've got a bad feeling about this," Brad said.

"Yeah. Me too." T.J. squared his shoulders and prepared himself for more drama. Seemed like there was a lot of that lately.

Chapter Four

They found their family in the dining room with white Chinese takeout cartons arranged in the center of the table. Brad and T.J. slid across from each other into the remaining two chairs.

Tantalizing aromas of everyone's favorites lingered in the air—fried rice, golden chicken fingers, sesame chicken, beef with mixed vegetables, lo mein noodles, and French fries. Their father occupied his old spot at one end, listening to Jory chatter about his class's ice cream sundae party for filling the good behavior marble jar. Mom stood at the other end, scooping noodles onto paper plates. She had laid out a snowy white tablecloth bordered with a red ribbon and Christmas trees.

Guilt sliced through Brad at Chris and Jory's grins. No way was this a happy family dinner after what he and T.J. learned last weekend. Usually their mother limited takeout. With everybody's hectic schedules, she would prepare batches of spaghetti sauce, meatloaf, and lasagna on Sundays and freeze them to defrost later. Other times she would leave pot roast, stew, or chili in the slow cooker while she was at work.

As enticing as this Chinese food smelled, it reeked of trouble. Brad gave his parents points for eating together and presenting a unified front, but a divorce announcement would devastate Chris and Jory.

During the meal, Mom kept springing up to fill cups and fetch napkins from the kitchen, worry lines creasing her forehead.

Once they'd finished, and the younger boys were about to drag their father into the living room, she motioned for them to sit back down. She perched on the edge of her chair. "There's something we need to talk to you about."

Even though Brad sensed where this was going, he still dreaded it.

"What's going on?" Chris asked.

Out of all the boys, Brad thought Chris resembled their father the most, inheriting Dad's chestnut hair and blue eyes that became piercing whenever he got upset. Which would happen any minute.

Mom released a breath. "You know Dad and I have been having problems. We've tried to fix things, but it isn't working out."

Blinking rapidly, Jory ping-ponged his stare from one parent to the other. "What do you mean?"

"We'll always be your mom and dad," their father said. "But we've decided not to be husband and wife anymore. Your mother and I are getting a divorce."

"We both love you kids very much," Mom added. "Even though we aren't staying married, we have children together. We're still a family."

A muscle pulsed in Brad's jaw. It sounded like they had memorized a clichéd script for how to tell your kids you were getting divorced.

Chris jerked his head up, his eyes in full piercing mode. "How? This is the first time we've all had dinner together in months. How is that being a family?"

"You're right," Dad acknowledged. "This has been new territory for us. It's a difficult transition, but we'll get through it."

"You're great kids," Mom assured them. "This is our fault. Not yours."

"What happened to trying to work out your differences?" His voice escalating, Chris gestured toward his brothers. "When we fight, you're always telling us to work it out. You're just giving up."

"You can't choose your siblings," she said softly. "Friends change over the years, but you'll always be brothers. It's important that you can rely on each other. You choose your partner though, and your father and I have drifted apart. We're all sad about this transition, but sometimes difficult decisions need to be made in life."

Under the table, Brad's fist clenched as tight as his stomach. If he heard *transition* one more time, Chris wouldn't be the only one yelling. How could they sound so calm and detached? Jory had tears sliding down his cheeks.

"You think this is what's best? I hate you for doing this. I hate you both." Chris jumped up and stormed around the corner to the stairs.

"Can't you just live together?" Jory pleaded, his chin quivering. "For me?"

"No, Jory," Dad said. "I'm afraid not. But I'm not even fifteen minutes away. You can come over anytime."

"Can I be excused?" Jory mumbled.

"Sure. I'll stop in to see you before I leave."

Brad watched his little brother shuffle upstairs after Chris. Part of him wanted to escape also, but when was the next time both his parents would share a table? T.J. hadn't left either. So he waited.

"We thought we should tell them now so you two wouldn't have to keep it a secret anymore." Their mother faltered. "I . . . I expected it to be hard, but that was awful."

"They'll be okay," Dad said. "Chris had a point though. We need to get together more often so the kids can talk to us both and have us on the same page."

"I agree," she replied, sounding a little stronger. "Since we're all here, do either of you boys have anything to bring up?"

"I have something. Barbara, are you really okay with Thomas putting college on hold to play hockey?"

All Brad's senses went on high alert, and he wished he'd gotten out of there when he had the chance.

"Yes. I am." Mom's sharp voice cut across the room. "The twins have done an amazing amount of research. They know what they need to do, and they're proactive about reaching out to college coaches. They're considering excellent schools and have attracted genuine interest. If it doesn't work out and they don't receive athletic scholarships, they'd just go to college a little later than their classmates."

Go, Mom. Brad's heart warmed at her staunch defense even as trepidation surged through him. An explosion was inevitable. Who would be the first to blow? Mom, Dad, or T.J.?

Dad's face reddened and he steepled his fingers onto the table. "There's no need for him to wait until he's nineteen or twenty to enroll in college. That's absurd."

"It's not like T.J will sit in his room and play video games. He'll be working hard and having a unique experience he'll remember his whole life."

"He might be the class valedictorian. Have you ever heard of a valedictorian who postponed college to play hockey?"

T.J. bolted to his feet. "Yeah, Dad, I read about a kid who became valedictorian while playing junior in Canada, attending high school away from home. The local papers interviewed him. But nothing's ever good enough for you, is it? I'm sick of you trying to control everything I do."

"You're my son and you're making a huge mistake."

"But Brad isn't? How is that fair? He's as smart as I am, just lazier."

"Hey," Brad protested, not sure whether to be flattered or insulted.

While insulted was winning, he wasn't too outraged. T.J. had a right to resent him. Dad wasn't involved in Brad's recruiting endeavors, not like typical hockey dads with a passion for the game and their sons' pro aspirations, but his father never lectured him about junior.

"Come on, you know it's true," T.J. said. "You didn't pull up your grades till you read the NCAA requirements."

"I wouldn't call it lazy—just unmotivated." Maybe it was the writer in him, but Brad didn't appreciate the negative connotations.

"Whatever!" T.J. turned back to their father, his gaze steely. "You've got no say in this, Dad. It's my decision. Not yours. I'm playing hockey next fall." He stalked out of the room and up the stairs. His door slammed.

That was Brad's cue to leave. He wasn't staying down here alone with his parents glowering at each other. He scraped back his chair against the hardwood floor. "Good talk, guys. Way to clear the room."

They both ignored him, not registering his sarcasm. Brad was halfway up the staircase when his mother demanded, "Why do you do that? Why do you have to be so controlling? Just because your father was controlling doesn't mean you have to be. Do you want to drive a wedge between them again? They're finally getting along and you have to treat them differently."

Brad paused to listen, his palm on the banister. Grandpa was controlling? He'd died when Brad was little and he barely remembered his grandfather.

"They're two different kids with different strengths! Thomas excels academically, he always has, so why encourage him to waste more time on a hobby that might go nowhere?"

"Stop calling him Thomas! He hates that and so do I. In fact, I wish we'd never named him after you."

Coldness crept over Brad and lodged in his gut. How could his mother say something that callous? At least T.J. hadn't overheard the remark. Swallowing hard, he trudged to the second floor, for the first time truly recognizing how much his parents brought out the worst in each other.

Let's see, what else had he learned tonight? Mom and Dad's

united front was bull. T.J. resented him. Chris was hanging out with McCann and developing a major attitude. And Jory hoped their parents could be roommates.

Great. Sounded like they were in for a pleasant holiday season. Instead of *The Twelve Days of Christmas*, they should change it to the *The Twelve Days of Dysfunction*.

Brad hesitated in the hallway outside T.J. and Chris's closed doors. Those two were so furious that they'd attack whoever was dumb enough to approach them. Nope, he was staying away until they cooled off. But Jory's door stood ajar, and he heard sniffling from inside.

Brad stepped into the room and swept his gaze around the walls. A handful of stuffed animals poked out from the bottom of the closet. Jory was still so young. Matchbox cars and Star Wars action figures filled bins on the shelves while graphic novels stacked a bookcase. In the corner lay mini sticks and a foam ball that he and his friends used for playing knee hockey in the hallway with the doorways as goals.

Jory sat with his back against the headboard, hugging his knees. His team pictures and posters of NHL players decorated the walls. Brad wished he and his little brother were at the rink doing sprints with their blades carving into the ice, problems melting as they focused on tearing back and forth under the lights.

He sank onto the Boston Bruins comforter and tapped Jory's foot, clad in a white sock. "You all right?"

"I don't want them to get divorced," Jory murmured.

"Neither do I, Jor, but we got through the separation and we'll get through this. Things won't be any different than they've been for the past year."

"I didn't like the past year." Jory's mouth flexed into a stubborn line.

Brad searched his brain for something reassuring to offer. All he could summon was Coach Reynold's locker room speech after the team got eliminated in the state finals. The guys had radiated gloom, hunched over with wet hair, sweaty grim faces, and their heads hanging.

"Remember when Bayview lost by one goal in the Super Eight? My coach told us that every bump, bruise, and loss on the ice makes you stronger and that when you hit rock bottom, you've got to have the courage to try again and know your team will have your back." Brad checked his brother's reaction. Jory was listening intently. "T.J, Chris, and me—we've got your back. When you're down, come find one of us."

"Chris is always grumpy." Jory's voice trembled. "And you're leaving next year. You and T.J."

Brad tamped down a swell of emotion. Jory appeared so vulnerable, a contrast to when he dominated the ice as his team's star forward. He played center like T.J., exhibiting his older brother's strength on face-offs, speed, and talent on defense and offense. It would be strange not seeing Jory every day and having the kid hound him to play games, talk hockey, or drive him somewhere.

"Hey, we'll still be in touch all the time. You can't get rid of me that easily."

"Promise?"

"You bet. Anyway, let's not worry about that right now. That's still a long way off." Brad forced a grin. "So, what's on your Christmas list? Any Lego sets we can work on?"

He left Jory's room a few minutes later, having given his younger brother every ounce of cheer that he could muster. It left Jory more upbeat and Brad drained. He ran into Chris in the hallway, coming out of the bathroom.

"You knew," Chris said flatly. "You and T.J. knew about this, and you didn't tell me."

"What're you talking about?"

"I overheard Mom say you were keeping it a secret."

"Just since last weekend. We asked Dad when he dropped us

off. We didn't plan to—it just happened. You were already inside."

"You guys should've told me." Belligerence—and hurt—shadowed Chris's words.

"Chris, it wasn't our place. That was up to Mom and Dad. Besides, it wasn't a shock, was it? Didn't you figure it was coming?"

"Yeah . . . I guess."

Brad sensed the defiance leaving his brother. "So are we cool?" He would let the McCann stuff go for now. Pursuing it when Chris was emotional would invite trouble.

"Yeah. It's just . . . it was a lousy night." Chris brushed past him and into his bedroom at the end of the hall.

After he shut off his light, Brad couldn't fall asleep. His mind kept jumping from his family, to Sherry, to where he would play junior and what it would be like. Restless, he rolled over for at least the twentieth time. He would work off his nervous energy during his morning workout and on the rink after school. That would distract him. He hoped. Brad didn't want another sleepless night.

Chapter Five

It was his fault his parents were divorcing. T.J. rejected the nagging thought while he and Brad perspired through a series of back squats, front squats, hang cleans, lunges, seated rows, and dumbbell shoulder presses in their basement workout room, but it kept returning.

How many times had Mom and Dad argued over his hockey aspirations? The brothers didn't mention the previous evening, both absorbed in their strength training as they cranked up a playlist full of powerful guitar and bass riffs and beating drums.

That afternoon at practice, T.J. tuned out his worries while he focused on practicing pivots, backwards crossovers, dekes, front fakes, tipping shots, and slapshots. He was in the zone, outperforming his teammates except for Brad and Chris who seemed equally on fire. Coach Reynolds and Coach Ryan observed in their winter hats and sweats, calling praise like, "Nice shot, McKendrick!" and "That's it, McKendrick, good one."

T.J. wasn't always sure which McKendrick they meant, but it didn't matter. It felt good skating with his brothers, having the same outlet for their frustrations. Chris had probably earned himself some shifts in tomorrow night's game. He gave T.J. and Brad high fives when they all combined for a goal.

His siblings wouldn't high-five him once they figured out T.J. caused their parents' divorce. He'd suspected it for a while, but always dismissed the idea. His parents argued over lots of things, not just him. But they'd disagreed over his future countless times, their debates growing more heated as graduation neared. He'd put them over the edge, increasing the tension in their marriage to the point that they couldn't go back. Hearing them argue again last night, T.J. was sure of it.

After practice, while T.J. unlaced his skates in the locker room, an idea hit him. His father's main concern about junior was failing to get a scholarship. If T.J. landed a verbal commitment now, even to attend college two years down the line, then that should satisfy his father. His parents would have no reason to fight over him. It wouldn't save their marriage, but it would save his sanity. Instead of giving 100 percent on the ice, he'd give 120 percent and do his best to reel in an offer.

"Hey, T.J., I'm having some of the seniors over tonight," said Russ, a defenseman with short red hair. "You in?"

"Thanks, but I have plans with Kayla," T.J. answered.

"Bring her. Brad and Sherry are going, right, Brad?" Russ asked.

"Yeah, come on, Teej," Brad urged. "It'll be fun."

T.J. supposed that after the turmoil last night, they both could use some fun. At least Brad didn't hold a grudge and wanted him to come. Last December, T.J's laziness comment would have led to a brawl.

"Yeah, come on, McKendrick," Trey echoed, wiping his glistening face with a towel. "Text Kayla and ask if she can bring a friend."

"Would that be a female friend?" T.J. hitched up a brow.

"Damn straight. No offense, but I talk to you guys enough."

"The feeling's mutual, Arenson," Brad interjected, tossing his practice jersey at Trey.

Coughing, Trey flung it back to him. "Geez, McKendrick, take a shower."

Coach Reynolds had a strict policy barring phone use in the locker room, but once he was outside, T.J. texted Kayla. Maybe a night bantering with his teammates would cheer him up. Besides, the later he stayed out, the less chance he'd run into his father. Dad was taking Chris and Jory to dinner and bowling. Afterward, Jory would sleep over at the condo, but since Bayview had an afternoon game tomorrow, Chris would get dropped off at home. T.J. didn't intend to be anywhere near the house.

Okay, as long as there's no drinking, Kayla texted back.

Don't worry, it's Russ.

But a few hours later, T.J. had to circle Russ's neighborhood and park further down the street. Several unfamiliar cars crammed the driveway and lined the sidewalk. Brad and Sherry had driven with him and Kayla while Alexis, Kayla's friend, rode with Trey. They'd met for burgers and then headed over to join Russ who apparently was hosting the party of the year.

Sherry frowned as they climbed the porch steps. "Who are all these people?"

"Russ's brother is home from college," Brad said. "Their parents are away."

"You couldn't have mentioned this?" T.J. asked. "I promised Kayla there wouldn't be drinking."

Kayla nodded in agreement and crooked her arms over her varsity jacket. "I'm not into this kind of scene."

"Neither am I," Sherry said.

"Will you guys relax?" Brad rapped on the front door. "How do you know what kind of scene it is? We're not even inside yet."

Russ greeted them, holding a red solo cup. Loud music and the smell of beer assaulted them. The girls shifted uncomfortably, and T.J. grimaced. If student-athletes got caught drinking, they lost eligibility for several games. He'd attended parties where alcohol turned up, but T.J. had learned whose houses to avoid. Russ's wasn't one of them.

"Russ, what the hell?" T.J. demanded, not budging from the porch. "If Coach or the principal hears about this—"

"You guys don't have to drink. My brother's friends are in the basement. There's plenty of soda and chips and stuff upstairs."

"Is that what you've got there?" T.J. gestured toward the cup brimming with beer. "A Coke?"

"This is the only one I'm having. And the other guys are in my room, playing video games. They're just eating junk food, I swear."

"T.J., lighten up," Brad cut in. "We'll hang out upstairs."

T.J. stared at his brother—his co-captain—who should be more concerned. "What if the neighbors call the cops?"

"I'm with T.J." Sherry clasped the railing, which was draped with a garland and a string of white lights. "We're underage. Can't we get blamed just by being here?"

"You can't even hear any noise from the street," Brad said. "If things get out of hand, we'll take off. There's Trey and Alexis."

Brad elbowed past Russ into the house, leaving his friends behind. T.J. couldn't believe his brother was barging in despite his girlfriend's reservations. Well, he'd be a nice guy even though Brad was acting like a jerk.

"Want me to take you home?" T.J. asked the girls. "I can come back for him later."

"I'll stay," Kayla responded after a hesitation. "For now. Since you're not drinking."

"I guess I will too," Sherry said. "But if it gets bad, we're out of here."

They joined Brad, Trey, and Alexis in the living room and started a comedy movie. Clapping and cheering erupted from the basement, making it difficult to hear. When Brad left to play video games, Sherry seemed tense, constantly checking the time on her phone. T.J. shook his head. First, Brad ignored her misgivings about the party, and now he was ditching her.

Once the movie ended, Sherry texted Brad that they were ready to go home. After he didn't respond to several messages, she rose from the couch. "I'll go pull him away from whatever they're playing."

"Good luck with that," Trey said, his muscular arm around

Alexis's petite shoulders.

T.J. was throwing out their snack wrappers in the adjoining kitchen when Sherry trudged in and informed him, "Brad wasn't with the guys. They said he, Russ, and Matt went downstairs a long time ago."

Great. There was only one reason to go down there. He'd never known Brad to drink, but then again, sometimes his twin acted reckless. None of the team members had better be drinking. Even if they didn't get caught, they had a game tomorrow.

"You don't think they're drinking, do you?" Sherry asked, on the same wavelength.

"I'll see what's going on. Trey, we've got some teammates partying in the basement."

"Right behind you, McKendrick," Trey said. "I'd better not have a bunch of hungover morons bumping into each other in the D-zone tomorrow."

They headed down the hall, passing a boy puking in the bathroom. When T.J. opened the basement door, the sounds of music and cheering intensified. He walked down the carpeted steps, Trey on his heels.

At the foot of the stairs, T.J. paused and took in the couples making out in dark corners, people crashed on the floor, and the guys downing vodka shots at the bar. Finally he sighted the ping-pong table toward the back of the room, Brad and Russ on one side and Matt opposite them. At each end, red solo cups formed a triangle.

Terrific. Since Matt was his other linemate, T.J. would have to endure sloppy play on both left and right wing.

Trey cursed. "You've got to be kidding me."

Brad aimed a white ball toward the cups. T.J. strode over and pried it from his brother's hand. "Seriously? You care more about beer pong than the game tomorrow?"

"Hey, I'm not done yet." Brad lunged for the ball.

Trey pushed himself in between the twins. "Trust me, *Captain,* you're done," he said, and fixed his glare on an amused Russ and Matt. "Let's go. I don't care if you puke your guts up tonight, you three better be on the ice tomorrow."

His firm tone quieted Matt, but Russ snorted with laughter. "I think they're mad at us."

"So what?" Brad picked up a cup and drank a long swallow of beer.

T.J. fished his cell phone out of his pocket and opened the camera. "How'd you like a picture of this sent to Coach Reynolds?"

"You wouldn't do that," Brad scoffed. "You need me feeding you the puck."

Anger surged through T.J. He was just trying to keep Brad out of trouble, and the idiot was totally ungrateful. Telling the coach would lead to missed games and scouts hearing about the incident. T.J. wouldn't risk Brad's future, however his jackass twin didn't need to know that. "I can score with or without you, so don't even go there. Either you come with us now or Reynolds, Mom, and Dad find out about this."

"You're bluffing," Brad said, but he lowered the cup to the table.

"You really want to take that chance, McKendrick?" Trey responded. "Here's how it's going down. You're all gonna get sobered up enough to make it past your parents. We're taking Matt's keys and he's riding home with me. When you wake up tomorrow, you all damn well be ready to play hockey."

"What'll I tell my parents about the car?" Matt whined.

"I don't know, say you lost your keys, or aliens stole it. Start thinking. Now let's go."

T.J. and Trey steered Russ up to his bedroom and told their other teammates it was time to leave. They coerced Brad and Matt outside, where they drank bottled water and huddled on the concrete front steps, breathing in the cold fresh air and mocking the inflatable Santa on the neighbor's lawn. Then Brad stumbled to his feet, pale, leaned over, and hurled in the bushes. That prompted Matt to do the same thing.

Cringing, T.J. spun the other way and found himself face-to-face with Sherry shivering in the shadows. "Hey, it's freezing out. You should wait in the car with Alexis and Kayla."

She tapped her foot against the grass, fidgeting. "I just needed some air. I'm furious at Brad, but I'm worried too. This isn't like him."

T.J. could relate. He wanted to throttle his brother, yet underneath his aggravation lay concern.

"I'm wondering if he's upset because of me," she went on. "That's why I agreed to stay at this stupid party, because I felt guilty. The other day he asked if I'd consider a college in New England." She paused, as if fearing his reaction. "I said no."

T.J. hoped she didn't pick up on his relief. He liked Sherry, but Brad was getting too dependent on her. "He brought that up? I told him that wasn't a good idea."

"Some of my friends thought he was being romantic. They were criticizing me for turning him down."

"Sherry, you've got to do what's right for you. It's not romantic if you're both making a big sacrifice. Besides, that's not the only thing on his mind. The recruiting pressure and not knowing where we'll be playing next year stresses me out, so I'm sure it's the same for him. And he must have told you about the divorce."

She blinked several times. "Your parents are getting divorced? No, he didn't. How long have you known?"

"Since last weekend. They told Chris and Jory last night. It didn't go so well." Interesting that Brad neglected to tell his girlfriend. T.J. had mentioned it to Kayla.

"I'm sorry. I know you guys were expecting it, but it still must have been hard." Sherry eyed Brad again. "But he should've been smart enough not to get smashed."

"I'll give him a hard time tomorrow, and I'm sure you will too. He'd be stupid to do it again."

"Thanks, T.J. He's lucky to have you."

"Trust me, he won't think so tomorrow."

It was midnight before T.J. finally parked in the garage. He had texted his mother that they were on the way, dropped off Kayla and Sherry, and gave Brad a breath mint, not that it helped much.

"Stay here," T.J. ordered. "Mom's probably reading in bed. I'll tell her you're behind me and that should satisfy her. I'll text you when it's safe to come up. Think you can handle that?"

"Stop treating me like you're better than me," Brad shot back, his speech slurred. "Why do you have to be so perfect all the time?"

"Perfect? It's taking all my strength not to strangle you right now."

T.J. slammed his car door and passed the wood pallet that corralled a dozen hockey sticks. Beside the pallet, Chris's gear hung on one of the metal racks for drying out equipment. If anyone had a late night game and early practice, a running fan would help with the wetness. It took lots of air freshener to make the garage odor tolerable. Too bad it wouldn't work on Brad to make his attitude more tolerable, not to mention the stench of beer, vodka, and vomit.

When T.J. got upstairs, his mother called from her bedroom, "Boys?"

He nudged open her door. She sat propped up against a backrest in a flannel nightgown, e-reader tablet in her lap. "Hey, Mom. We're back."

"Did you have a good time?"

"It was okay. Want me to turn off your light?"

"Sure, thanks." She moved her tablet to her nightstand. "Where's Brad?"

"He'll be up in a minute. He was thirsty." *Way too thirsty.* "I'd better get to bed. We're playing Fremont tomorrow."

T.J. switched off the light and closed the door behind him. He texted Brad and waited beside a wall of framed school pictures.

Once he made sure his twin didn't break his neck on the stairs, Brad was on his own.

He heard movement from Chris's room, and T.J.'s younger brother appeared in the doorway in an old travel hockey T-shirt and a pair of sweats. Just then, Brad answered the text with a series of misspelled words that T.J. deciphered as "I'm coming now" but that resembled a secret code with all the extra letters in between.

"Who's texting you this late?" Chris asked.

"Trey." T.J. cast a glance down the stairs. He didn't want Chris getting any ideas about drinking. "Why don't you go back to bed?"

Too late. Brad clambered up the steps and slung his arm around their kid brother's shoulders. "Hey! It's Christopher! Little M! What's up, little bro?"

A delighted grin crept across Chris's face. "No way! Are you—"

"Ssh," Brad stage-whispered in his ear. "I'm sneaking in."

"That's it. Let's go." T.J. gave him a hard push toward his room and motioned for Chris to follow.

When they were inside, Brad mumbled something to Chris. They both snickered as they looked at T.J., probably making fun of how uptight he was. T.J. snagged a pair of earbuds off the nightstand and tossed them to his twin, who not surprisingly missed the catch. "Get in bed, listen to some music, and be quiet. I'm not covering for you anymore tonight. Chris, come on."

"But this is hilarious," Chris protested. "I want to see what he does next."

"He already puked once. Trust me, you don't want to see round two."

Chris wrinkled his nose. "Gross. Night, Brad."

After brushing his teeth, T.J. stopped in Chris's room. A golden halo spilled from the nightlight, breaking through the darkness. "What Brad did wasn't cool, okay?"

"Come on, it's not that big of a deal." Chris squinted up at him.

"Yes, it is. Tomorrow, he'll regret you seeing this." That much, T.J. knew for sure. He and Brad always watched out for their younger brothers.

"He screwed up big-time, Chris. If the school finds out, a first violation of the chemical health rule means missing the next several games, totaling 25 percent of all the games in the season." After talking to Sherry, T.J. had downloaded the athletic handbook from the Bayview High website, refreshing his memory. "That's at least five games, so it's not like he could hide it from the scouts. Do you think they want some immature kid with a rep for partying?"

"But he'll get away with it, right?" Chris asked. "The school won't find out?"

"I don't know. What he did was stupid and has consequences. Hopefully, this time it will just be a hangover and slower reflexes tomorrow." *But they'd better not be too slow.* "Don't you go out and try this."

"Okay, okay. You don't need to lecture me, Dad. Geez."

Sometimes, Chris acted like a younger version of Brad—stubborn and infuriating. Once again, anger shot through T.J. Not only was Brad setting a bad example for their brother and the rest of the team, but every game affected their future.

Chapter Six

Sunlight streaked through Brad's bedroom window, giving him an instant headache. His heart raced and queasiness rolled through his stomach. He needed to sleep this off, but someone kept rapping on his door, making his temples throb harder.

Reluctantly, Brad raised his head. "What?" he mumbled.

T.J. strode into the bedroom and slammed the door, jostling the attached basketball net. "You look like hell."

He stepped over a school-issued Chromebook and a stack of notebooks that contained Brad's latest horror story and his video production homework. Brad squinted through blurry vision at the hockey stick mounted on the wall with tournament medals dangling from it. Beside it, MVP and All Star trophies crowded a shelf. Those were his prouder moments. Unlike this one.

"I've got a hangover," he muttered.

"No kidding." T.J. shoved the homework papers, gaming headphones, and controllers off the desk chair, about to sit down until he noticed a filthy sock. He shook his head in disgust. Brad didn't blame him. He wouldn't want to touch it without gloves either.

T.J. kept standing, sipping something reddish brown and creamy that resembled milky ketchup. Brad's stomach twisted. That was the protein smoothie T.J. made on game days, a concoction of Greek yogurt, unsweetened almond milk, strawberries, almond butter, coconut oil, and coconut shavings. His brother was always after him to try it, but since Brad wasn't a Greek yogurt or coconut fan, it sounded nasty. Especially now. Once again, his stomach lurched.

"Do you have to drink that in here?" Brad averted his gaze and frowned at the ceiling fan revolving above them. Why was it spinning on high speed? He never used it in December. Oh. That was the room spinning.

"Why? Is it making you nauseous?" T.J. downed another long sip. "Here's an idea. Maybe you shouldn't have gotten wasted."

"It was a mistake. Get over it." Brad fell back against his pillow. Now black dots were dancing in front of him. He didn't know which was worse, the dizziness or watching T.J. chug that lumpy protein shake.

"Get over it? If the school hears about this, you'll sit out a quarter of the season. What the hell were you thinking? Do you think the scouts won't notice if you're suspended? You're in touch with some of them every week! Your first choice college is BC—a Jesuit Catholic university that doesn't even recognize fraternities or sororities."

"Okay, okay. I wasn't thinking, all right?"

"Yeah, I'll say. You'd better come up with something better than that for Sherry."

Brad didn't remember much about last night, but he could imagine her reaction. Worried and mad. Make that livid if T.J.'s attitude was any sign.

"Chris saw you too and thought you were pretty funny," T.J. continued. "I hope you're going to talk to him."

"Later. Now go away and let me sleep."

"We have a twelve o'clock game. You'd better pull yourself together before then." With another head shake, T.J. left the room.

Brad stole one more hour of restless slumber and then stumbled into the bathroom to shower. When he was getting dressed, he noticed a water bottle and a plate of crackers on his nightstand. T.J. must have put them there. Since his mother hadn't confronted him, he'd bet that T.J. had helped him last night too.

He owed his brother—and Sherry—an explanation. Not that

he knew what to tell them. Brad hadn't planned to get drunk. Okay, when Russ mentioned the party, it crossed his mind that a couple beers might relax him, but he hadn't meant for things to spiral out of control.

Before leaving for the rink, Brad called his girlfriend. He sat on his bed, back pressed against the wall. Every muscle in his body ached. This hangover was so not worth the few carefree hours he'd spent. "Sherry, I'm sorry."

"You should be," she responded, her tone chilly. "You were acting like another person."

"I'm sorry," he repeated.

"Why didn't you tell me that your parents were getting a divorce? Why did I have to hear about it from T.J.?" Her voice thawed a little.

How could he make her comprehend that he hadn't felt like it? That he wanted to forget his problems for one weekend, not analyze them to death? Sherry never hid her emotions though sometimes Brad wished she would. Whenever she fought with her mom, or one of her friends made a catty comment, he heard all about it. Over and over again. He would have revealed the news this week, but Sherry wouldn't understand his desire to avoid the topic for now.

"Maybe because T.J. has a big mouth," he said, peeved at his brother again. "I was going to tell you. I didn't get a chance."

"Come on, Brad, don't give me lame excuses. You had a chance to get drunk."

"I didn't mean for that to happen. I got caught up in the moment."

"You're telling me it had nothing to do with the divorce? Or me going to school in Florida?"

"Did you ever think that I just might like the taste of beer?" Brad snapped, fed up with her pushing him.

"So this is a new habit?" she demanded.

"No, come on. I'm not saying that."

"Well, you're not saying much. Good luck at your game. You're going to need it. By the way, I won't be there." Sherry clicked off, and Brad slumped his shoulders.

They'd had a couple heated arguments in the past, but she'd never hung up on him. *Sherry might break up with me over this.*

Though they would probably call it quits next year, anyway. If his parents couldn't mend their difficulties living fifteen minutes apart, how would he and Sherry manage with over a thousand miles between them?

"Brad, let's go!" T.J. shouted from the hallway.

Brad dragged himself off the bed, wondering how he would survive this game.

***

By the second period, Brad felt as if he had been run over by a Zamboni. With his sluggish reflexes, he kept letting opponents beat him to the puck. He'd attempted a few lousy passes, an irony that drew a sneer from McCann. Brad regretted insulting his passing that time at the pizza place.

"Better hope no scouts are out there," McCann said during a line change. "They'll think you went blind."

Brad's hungover linemate Matt wasn't playing any better and took a penalty for elbowing. Russ had called out sick, which riled Brad since he'd made it here. But skipping the game might have been a wise decision.

"Will you wake up?" T.J. demanded after Fremont scored thanks to Brad being out of position.

"I'm trying," Brad fired back. You'd think his own twin would cut him some slack.

"Try harder!" T.J. snapped.

Trey swept the puck out of the net, silent behind his goalie mask, and Brad swallowed a wave of guilt. Or was that nausea? Maybe a little of both.

When Brad skated to the bench for another line change, Coach Reynolds frowned. "McKendrick, you're not yourself today. I'm sitting you out."

T.J. muttered something that sounded like, "About time."

"Chris and Greg, you've done a good job on your shifts today. When T.J's line goes back out, you're taking over for Brad and Matt."

Chris's eyes widened, and Brad sensed his shock. Moving up to the first line was a huge deal for his little brother.

"You've got this," Brad assured him.

"Yeah, you can't do any worse," T.J. commented.

Too exhausted to argue, Brad watched the team battle to dig the puck out of the defensive zone. His parents and Jory were somewhere in the bleachers though he suspected his mother was near the other hockey moms, not with Dad. The stands behind the benches were roped off during high school games as parents and students would taunt the opposing players. He deserved some badgering. His family and the fans must wonder what was wrong with him. Everyone had an off game now and then, but this was his worst performance ever.

Between periods, the team huddled on the ice before the bench. Coach Reynolds pulled Brad aside, and they both moved to the vacant far end of the bench that typically housed the backup goalie and players who weren't taking shifts. They stood inside facing each other. "McKendrick, what's going on with you?"

Brad shifted under his coach's scrutiny. He could feign an illness, but Russ used that cover story, and Matt mentioned he was developing a sore throat to justify his own shoddy skating. Too much sickness after a Friday night and Coach Reynolds would get suspicious.

"Sorry, Coach, I'm just distracted with some personal stuff. I'll play better next game." Brad forced himself to make eye contact even though his guilt had doubled since they'd been talking.

"You're under a lot of pressure with the scouts. If you're

stressed, make sure you talk to someone. Coach Ryan and I will try to help any way we can."

"I will," Brad said, wishing this conversation were over. "Thanks."

Unfortunately, Coach Reynolds wouldn't let it go. "T.J.'s pretty tense out there. Everything okay at home?"

"Our parents are getting divorced."

A flash of understanding flickered across the coach's face as if that explained everything. "I'm sorry to hear that. It's a difficult situation, but do whatever it takes to deal with it off the ice so it doesn't affect your game. Or schoolwork. Your senior year is too important to let yourself get derailed. Can you handle going back out there?"

"I kind of have a headache. I don't want to cost us the game."

"All right. Make sure you buck up before the Christmas tournament. We can't afford to have you distracted again."

"I know." His coach left him alone, and Brad returned to his teammates clustered on the ice. Now he felt like two Zambonis had blindsided him.

Since they were down 2-0, Coach Reynolds delivered a rousing speech about how they had plenty of time left and needed to forget what had just happened. "Put it behind you," he advised the morose athletes milling in front of the bench. "Sometimes you have to fail before you succeed. Go out there and make it a hockey game. Let's win that opening draw and get after it. We've got to win one shift at a time."

T.J., Chris, and Greg took the advice to heart. While Brad watched from his new seat at the end of the bench, Greg pulled the puck back and directed it toward his linemates.

"Yours!" T.J. called.

Chris collected the pass, his stick blade covering the puck. A defenseman chased after him, bearing down on the freshman.

"Man on!" Brad yelled from the bench, warning Chris that he had company.

Chris spun the disk ahead of him to T.J., who approached the net one-on-one with the goalie, stickhandling side to side. T.J. faked a shot before going backhanded and burying the puck into the net.

Brad joined the team and the Bayview fans in celebrating. He didn't want a shutout loss tarnishing their record, and if they had a chance for a comeback, Brad didn't care who scored, even if it was his surly brother.

He predicted goal two when T.J. hooked the puck off a forward's stick and wheeled down the ice, one defender between him and the goalie. The defenseman backed up; T.J. darted behind the net. As the guy followed him, T.J. crossed in front of the goal and stuffed the puck past the goaltender.

With two minutes left in the period, T.J. scored a bar down game-winning goal on another assist from Chris, the puck pinging the crossbar over the goalie's shoulder and falling straight down over the goal line. Even as he clapped, a twinge of jealousy darted through Brad. T.J. had just gone bar down, which was one of the coolest shots in hockey, and scored a hat trick. Brad's absence hadn't slowed his twin brother at all. Not only that, Chris had gained his first varsity points as the left winger on *Brad's line*. He would have liked to contribute to that milestone.

After the game, once they changed out of their uniforms, T.J. curtly told him to find a ride home as he had plans with Kayla. Brad strode out of the locker room and located his family near the front entrance. His parents were praising Chris on a good game, with Jory between them as a buffer.

Brad's mother, in her winter hat, wool coat, and boots, regarded him with her lips narrowed into a thin line. Uh-oh. Had she somehow heard about last night?

"Brad, are you feeling okay?" Dad asked.

"I think I'm coming down with something," Brad said, going with his friends' excuse. Adjusting the equipment bag over his shoulder, he ignored Chris's smirk.

"You'd better rest up. You don't want a repeat performance like that for the Christmas tournament. Were any scouts here?"

Brad sure hoped not. "I don't think so."

"Where's your brother?" His father scanned the foyer, mostly occupied by the players' friends and families preparing to leave.

"He's around somewhere."

"Thomas, why don't you get going?" Mom suggested. "You can see T.J. tomorrow when you drop off the kids." The younger boys were spending the night at their father's place. When their dad texted Brad and T.J. that morning, inviting them to come too, they both declined. Brad just wanted his own room with privacy to sleep off his hangover.

"Okay, but I mean it, Brad," their father said. "Take care of yourself so you can get your strength back."

"I will." Brad gave Chris a fist bump, promised Jory he'd watch the Bruins game with him tomorrow night, and then he and his mother were left alone. Not acknowledging him, she lowered her head and started texting. Her phone chirped with a reply and she tapped out a quick response.

When T.J. and Kayla walked over a minute later, Brad figured out who she had been texting.

"Why do I need to come home?" T.J. asked. "We're going to a movie."

"Because I have to talk to you. It's okay to drive Kayla home, but then I need you at the house."

Brad exchanged a quick glance with his brother, the twin telepathy coming through loud and clear. He was getting the "I'm going to kill you" vibe from T.J.

Mom turned to Kayla, who wore a Bayview High softball sweatshirt and jeans. "I'm sorry to cancel your plans on such short notice."

"That's okay, Mrs. McKendrick. Come on, T.J., let's go so you can get home." Kayla slipped her hand into his and they started toward the exit.

A few minutes later, Brad climbed into his mother's cold mini-van. Her vinyl *Hockey Mom* bumper sticker had a puck replacing the "o" in hockey. As soon as the doors were closed, she faced him, her expression grave. "Matt's mother took me aside and told me he came home drunk last night. He claimed you and Russ were drinking. Is that true?"

Mouth dry, Brad jammed his hands into his jacket pockets. "Yeah."

"I thought so. Once I saw how you were playing, I figured she was right. Why did you do it?"

"I don't know."

"Come on, Brad. Were your friends pressuring you? Were you curious? Is it because of the divorce?"

She'd obviously been running every scenario through her mind. Brad sighed and stared through the windshield at the parking lot. She wanted to dissect his feelings. He didn't. "I guess I was curious."

"This isn't like you." Mom raked her fingers through her blonde waves. "Sherry wasn't drinking, was she?"

"No. Trey and T.J. weren't either." He rested his head against the window, wondering if this was what a migraine felt like. "They were upstairs watching TV, and we were in the basement. They didn't know what we were doing until they came looking for us."

"So, when T.J. stopped in to see me last night, he was covering for you."

Brad straightened in his seat. "Don't be too hard on him. He didn't want to go to the party, but I talked him into it, and he dragged me out of there. He's been a real pain about it all day." Even though T.J. was acting obnoxious, he had done nothing wrong. Well, lying, but that wasn't as bad as drinking. They didn't deserve the same punishment. Besides, if T.J. got grounded, then he'd be even more impossible.

Mom started the car and fiddled with the heater. "I'll take that under consideration."

When Brad and his mother got home, they waited for T.J. in the living room. Brad stretched out on the couch, closing his eyes until the garage doors rumbled. It took a few minutes for T.J. to enter the house. He was probably hanging his gear and delaying this as long as possible.

Finally, he came in and dropped onto the loveseat beside his mother. "What's going on?"

"Does sneaking your brother into the house last night sound familiar?" Mom asked.

His face remained stoic. "I wasn't drinking."

"Brad told me that. So did Matt's mother." She leaned over and touched T.J.'s knee. "I'm grateful that you made sure Brad was safe. And I'm proud of you for not drinking and being a responsible driver. But there's a fine line between being a caretaker and an enabler."

"I didn't enable him."

"By keeping it from us, that's exactly what you were doing. Your father and I need to know when something like this happens. What if Brad did this again, and you weren't around to bail him out? Lots of things can happen when someone is drunk. I used to work at a hospital, guys." She removed her hand from T.J's leg and twisted her gold watch. "Teenagers have drowned in two feet of water. A few years ago, a boy bled to death after smashing his fist through a window and wandering off. I'm glad you were watching out for your brother, but keeping it a secret was putting too much responsibility on yourself."

"It won't happen again," Brad said. "I only drank because T.J. was my ride home."

"Great, thanks," T.J. said sarcastically.

Mom spoke before Brad could hurl back a retort. "You need to understand my point. Your friends didn't even know where you were. Just because you're in the house doesn't mean you're safe."

She transferred her worried gaze from Brad to T.J. "I want to feel secure that if either of you are ever in trouble, like if you didn't have a ride home, Brad, that you'll call your father or me. We'll come and get you, wherever you are. We love you boys and what we care about more than anything is your safety. Do you promise you'll be honest with us? And with your billet families when you're playing junior?"

They both nodded. A lump bobbed in Brad's throat. He hadn't meant to upset his mother. She had enough on her plate between work and the divorce.

"You're both grounded for the rest of the weekend. No going out and no technology. Brad, you can expect to be grounded much longer, but I need to discuss it with your father."

"Are you telling Coach Reynolds? That could ruin Brad's chances with the scouts." T.J. sounded concerned which slightly cheered Brad that his brother still cared.

"Matt's mother and I agree that since this has only happened once, it should be a family matter and handled privately. She's calling Russ's parents too." Mom rose and addressed Brad who was still lying down with his head on the throw pillow. "If this gets on the school's radar, you'll have to accept their punishment. We signed something about alcohol and substance abuse at the pre-season meeting, remember? I hope they don't find out, because you're a good kid and I think the divorce was a factor, but that was the chance you took."

Brad's chest tightened. He was pretty sure things would be okay. It wasn't like a bunch of classmates were snapping pictures and posting them online, and his teammates wouldn't want him missing games. Still, it would take a while to lose the fear of game suspension.

"We'll talk more about this later. I'm going to get dinner ready." Mom flipped the wall switch to illuminate the Christmas tree and disappeared into the kitchen.

Brad shaded his hand over his eyes to block the flashing lights.

T.J. stood, probably to go study so he would ace another test. *Or to take a hockey stick and trash my room.* Brad sat up and hunched forward, lacing his fingers together, knowing he owed his twin an apology. If he wanted to break the tension between them, then he'd have to make the first move.

"Sorry I got you into this, bro. Thanks for being there for me last night."

T.J. didn't answer right away, then he shrugged and cracked a small smile. "Believe me, I was tempted to knock you out cold so you'd shut up."

"No kidding. I thought you were gonna drop the gloves and take a swing at me today."

"Is that still an option?"

Brad tossed a pillow at him. T.J. ducked, and it smacked into the tree, dislodging a few ornaments. They both snickered, and T.J. looped the hangers back onto the branches. "You'd better watch out, or you'll get coal in your stocking."

"After last night, that's probably a done deal," Brad said, relieved they were joking with each other again.

"Yeah. About that." T.J.'s grin evaporated. "Why did you take that risk?"

"I guess I needed a break from the pressure."

"You can't afford another 'break.' This season is too important."

"You don't have to remind me."

"You know who else will remind you? Dad. He'll go nuts when Mom tells him about this."

"It might distract him from how you'll be wasting your life in junior. You should thank me." Brad collapsed against the back cushion, weary again.

"I wouldn't go that far," T.J. said. "But I wouldn't mind you taking some heat for a change. No offense."

Brad lumbered to his feet, glad he'd made up with T.J. but burned out from talking. Especially about how much trouble he was in. "See you tomorrow for the next parental lecture. I'm going to bed."

So what if it was only five o'clock? With any luck, he'd wake up in the morning and this would all be a nightmare.

Chapter Seven

T.J. hadn't been in his father's old home office in months. It had the same furniture as last fall when his parents announced they were pulling him from Hayden Prep for financial reasons—the same computer and printer, imposing mahogany desk, black swivel chair, tall bookcases, and leather couch. However, now his mother's exercise bike and yoga mat filled the the corner, and she'd added bins of glue sticks, construction paper, highlighters, pens, scissors, and markers to the shelves. School supplies for whoever needed them. Big rolls of snowman and poinsettia wrapping paper leaned upright against the wall.

Before, the office had been Dad's space, but he'd set up a smaller work area at the condo and this one had become obsolete. Jory did his homework at the desk and had left behind geography study sheets, tests marked with 100 and "Great Job" across the top, and a box of colored pencils. To T.J., it seemed surreal sitting here parked beside Brad on the couch with Mom on a folding chair and Dad behind the desk.

"Brad, what were you thinking? I can't believe you jeopardized everything for a party. And now you've put your mother and me into this unethical situation of lying to the school." Frustration rang in Dad's voice as he glared across the room at his sons. Even though their father spoke to Brad, he directed the glare at both of them.

"It's not lying," Brad said, a baseball cap tucked down over his forehead. "Besides, it's not like you ever talk to my coaches or teachers. You barely come to any games."

T.J. hadn't expected him to get defensive. He thought Brad would admit his mistake and try to placate Dad, but his brother was giving off a major attitude. He sat slouched in a concert T-shirt with his arms crossed and blue-jeaned legs extended on the ottoman, sending the glare right back.

The corners of Dad's mouth pinched together into a deeper frown. "In case you forgot in your hungover state, I came to a game yesterday. Most of the time, I'm working, since I'm supporting four sons who play one of the most expensive sports there is."

He was also a workaholic though their father would never admit it. They'd had recent money struggles, and to help with hockey fees, both twins had gotten summer jobs—T.J. as a lifeguard and Brad as a camp counselor. But Dad prioritized his architectural firm over family long before they had financial issues. When he was a kid, T.J. gave up asking his father to spend time with him. He was always too busy.

"Anyway, that's not the point. Why on earth would you do something so irresponsible?" Dad zeroed in on T.J. "And you! Just being at that party was a risk. I don't understand your judgment."

"You said you wanted to talk to them, not yell," Mom cut in. "I already explained that T.J. stayed so Brad would have a ride. He got Brad home safely. Would it kill you to commend him on the positive instead of just focusing on the negative?"

"Neither one of them should have been there. I already told you that we should ground Thomas for longer, but you'll do what you want no matter what I say." His tone dripped with a rancor that chilled T.J. Once again, his parents were arguing about him. Would it ever end?

Dad took a deep breath and turned back to T.J. When he spoke, he sounded more controlled though it didn't ease T.J.'s discomfort. "While I appreciate what you did, there were other options like texting us or calling."

"Do you both have a better understanding of what to do in a situation like that?" Mom asked.

The boys nodded. T.J. avoided looking at Brad so they wouldn't exchange eye rolls.

"Brad, we have a couple more things to discuss," Mom continued. "T.J., you can go now. You're not grounded anymore."

Dad didn't say anything, but gave an exasperated sigh. T.J. retreated to the living room where he found Jory immersed in his iPad and Chris scrolling through his phone, the television tuned to a hockey game.

"Well?" Chris asked. "What happened?"

"What do you think happened? Dad did a lot of yelling." T.J. headed to the stairs, his adrenaline running high and his thoughts whirling.

This day just kept getting worse and worse. First the stressful game, then on the ride home Kayla had invited him over for Christmas Eve and to her cousin's wedding in February. How serious did she think they were? You didn't ask someone you casually dated to attend a family holiday or wedding. He made up an excuse for Christmas and said he would check his schedule for February, not wanting to reject her twice in the same day. Now T.J. would have to break up with her in January. He'd rather not, but if she was going to get needy and put demands on his time, he had no choice. His father's reprimands and his parents' arguing capped one hell of a weekend.

"Did Brad really get drunk, and I missed it?" Grinning, Jory lowered his iPad. "Chris said it was funny. Next time, come and get me."

T.J. pivoted toward Chris, who was also grinning. "You were talking like that to a ten-year-old?"

"It's true, isn't it?"

"You didn't have to make getting drunk sound like a comedy routine. Don't you ever think about what comes out of your mouth?"

T.J. was tired of his parents fighting about him. Tired of his brothers doing whatever the hell they pleased while he was the responsible one. Tired of never being good enough for his father no matter how hard he tried.

"Geez, will you lay off?" Chris demanded. "It's not my fault you got in trouble."

"Yeah, come on, T.J., we were just kidding around," Jory said.

"Whatever. I don't care." T.J. stalked up to his room, knowing he should do his homework but too wired to focus. He eyed the pile of textbooks for AP Statistics, AP U.S. History, AP English Literature and Composition, and Forensic Science.

T.J. had two tests this week and a report to write. He'd heard Jenna Marcus, the girl ranked number one in the senior class, was having difficulty with AP Physics. His grades were nose-to-nose with Randy Keller, ranked number two.

If T.J. kept pushing himself, he had a real chance at surpassing them and making valedictorian. Just what Dad wanted for him. T.J. had wanted it too, but not anymore. Agitating his father would be far more rewarding.

He loaded the books into his backpack. He'd study for his AP exams in May to earn college credits and accelerated placement, but no more striving for the highest grade point average in the senior class.

I'm done living up to Dad's expectations.

He grabbed his car keys off the cleared desk. He'd run at the high school track, and when he returned, Dad should be gone. Then T.J. would spend the next couple hours practicing shots in the driveway and lifting weights.

Forget school. All that mattered was hockey. Getting a verbal commitment, getting Dad to quit butting into his life, and getting out of this house.

Chapter Eight

Brad flopped onto his bed with a soda and a package of peanut butter crackers, hoping eating would make him feel better. His parents' endless speeches had triggered a headache that rivaled the one from yesterday's hangover. Mom repeated the same points as if he were too dense to get it the first time, and Dad kept raising his voice and lamenting his disappointment.

Even worse, his mother insisted Brad needed to see a therapist and talk about his feelings. She planned to set up an appointment for after the holidays.

Sorry, Mom, I'm not spilling my guts to some shrink.

"Hey. Thanks a lot," Chris said, stepping into the room and resting his lean body against the doorframe.

Can't anyone in this family leave me alone for two minutes? Brad popped open his soda can, hoping Chris would make this quick. "What're you talking about?"

"I got stuck listening to a responsible drinking lecture. Mom and Dad are afraid I'll follow in your drunken footsteps."

That had worried Brad too, but he'd lacked the energy to deal with it. "What did you say?"

"That I'm not an idiot." Chris chuckled. "I mean, you and Matt got benched, and I got shifts on the first line."

"Thanks for the reminder."

"So, how long are you grounded?"

"Till after New Year's," Brad said.

They'd confiscated his cell phone and iPad, along with suspending his driving and TV privileges. His parents would allow Brad to use his Chromebook at school and for homework, but that was it. He had to come straight home after practice.

"That sucks," Chris said. "Want to play roller hockey? You can still do that, right?"

"I don't feel like it right now." Brad ripped open the crackers.

"Come on, I'm bored."

"So, get T.J. or Jory." Suddenly, Brad remembered he hadn't studied for his English test tomorrow. A study session sounded even less appealing than going outside with Chris, who would pester him for details about the party and getting grounded.

"T.J.'s being an ass, and Jory's doing his science project. Come on, afraid I'll outplay you?"

Brad thudded his soda can onto his nightstand. "Stop bugging me. Go annoy somebody else."

Chris stared at him and then muttered, "T.J.'s not the only who's being an ass. I've got better things to do, anyway." He slammed the door behind him.

Grimacing, Brad retrieved his English notebook from the carpet and ate a couple crackers. He reread the same highlighted notes five times, none of it sinking in, and gave up. A nap was a better plan. Brad was about to try that when T.J. burst into the room in a sweatshirt and sweatpants. Sweat gleaned on his face.

"Let's do drills in the driveway."

"I'm not feeling that great," Brad answered.

"Come on, the fresh air will wake you up." T.J. crossed to the window and raised the shade, which Brad hadn't bothered to open. Lucky for his brother, it wasn't a sunny day, the sky marbled with gray and white clouds.

"Play with Chris."

"Chris isn't my regular linemate and isn't talking to scouts. We've got to be ready for the tournament."

"We've got a whole week before it starts. Besides, I am ready."

"Are you kidding?" T.J. scoffed. "You got benched yesterday."

"I had a good reason." Well, maybe not a *good* reason.

"Yeah, your head isn't in the game." T.J. scooped a sweatshirt off the floor and threw it to him. "Let's go."

"Chris is right about your attitude," Brad muttered.

Reluctantly, he slid the sweatshirt over his T-shirt and trailed T.J. down to the garage. They fetched their old sticks, a couple shooting pads, and a bag of pucks and stickhandling balls. Soon, they each had a row of pucks lined up as obstacles and were practicing a push and pull drill in the space between the pucks—pushing the ball away from their bodies as if enticing an opponent and then pulling it back in using the toe of the blade.

"So, I'm grounded for two weeks," Brad said after a while, taking a break.

"You're lucky it wasn't longer." T.J. had progressed to backhand toe drags.

"Lucky? We're talking two weeks of no phone, iTunes, TV, or going out with my girlfriend."

If she's still my girlfriend, Brad thought.

"It'll give you time to practice and work out without distractions."

"Plus they want me to see a shrink."

"Lots of athletes go to sports psychologists." T.J.'s blade slapped against the slick surface as he continued with his seamless movements.

"This isn't a sports psychologist." Brad wondered why he'd expected empathy. Lately, T.J. focused on hockey 24/7, not caring about anything else.

"It'll still help your game if you get things off your mind."

"Then text Sherry and ask her to meet me in the cafeteria during support tomorrow. If she forgives me, that'll be one problem off my mind." During the twenty-minute support period, students could visit teachers for extra help, do makeup work, and meet for school projects and extracurricular activities, though most kids socialized in the cafeteria or library.

67

T.J. leveled a glance at him. "Sherry's one of the distractions. Maybe it wouldn't be such a bad thing if you two broke up."

Brad stared at him in disbelief. "Are you serious?"

T.J. tapped his stick hard against the shooting pad. "You can't even finish a drill without thinking about her. What'll happen when it's the state tournament and we're getting closer to graduation? Or next summer at training camp? Are you going to fall apart because Sherry's moving to Florida? She told me that you talked to her. And that she still wants to go."

Brad's head swam at the idea of his girlfriend and brother discussing this behind his back. He stepped toward T.J., prepared to shatter their truce from yesterday. "It's none of your business."

"It is if it affects your game."

"You can have a girlfriend, but I'm supposed to dump mine?"

"I'm probably breaking up with Kayla in January."

"Let me guess. She's getting too clingy."

"Yeah. So?"

"Just because you're crappy at relationships doesn't mean everyone is. Did you ever stop to think that maybe Kayla isn't the one with the problem?" Brad walked to the last puck on the mat and aimed it into the net. It smacked in along with the next three pucks that he fired. "My game is fine. So go to hell." He strode toward the front steps, leaving the equipment for T.J. to clean up.

"You're the one that'll wind up there if you don't get your act together—it's called Tier III!" T.J. shouted after him, referring to the pay-to-play junior leagues that charged for coaching, ice time, room and board, and more depending on the franchise.

When Brad set foot in the living room, Chris seemed ready to leave the house, wearing his jacket and counting the bills in his wallet.

"Guess you weren't too busy to play hockey with T.J.," Chris said, standing by the stupid blinking Christmas tree.

"Trust me, I regret getting talked into it. Where're you going?"

Wherever it was, Brad envied him. He wouldn't be going any-where for a while besides school, the rink, and to his father's place for Christmas Eve.

"The movies. With McCann." A smug smile hovered on Chris's lips.

Clearly, Brad's kid brother was angling to get a rise out of him. "You're not going anywhere with that loser," he warned.

"I don't have to listen to you. Besides, Mom already said yes."

"Chris, seniors don't hang around with freshmen. How can you be this naive?"

Their mother came downstairs and fetched her purse off a coat hook in the entryway. "Ready to go, Chris?"

"Mom, you can't let him go out with McCann," Brad said. "He's a bad influence."

"Bad influence?" Chris laughed. "You're joking, right? Aren't you grounded for sneaking in drunk?"

"All right, that's enough," their mother cut in. "Brad, we have to give Glen a chance. I've already told Chris that the only teenagers allowed to drive him around are you and T.J. I'll be dropping him off at the movies and picking him up. There's no need to worry."

"He's not worried. He just wants to boss me around." Chris stomped out to the garage.

Their mother paused with her hand on the back of the couch. "I know you're trying to help, but Chris has kept to himself a lot. The situation between your father and I has been hard on him. I'm glad he's found a friend on the team."

"McCann's not a real friend. He's up to something."

"For Chris's sake, I hope you're wrong, but he has to find that out for himself. Next year, he won't have you and T.J. around to protect him, and right now he's very much in your shadow. He's got to learn to make his own way." She touched Brad's shoulder. "T.J.'s outside with a hockey stick. Why don't you join him?"

"No thanks," he responded without thinking. "I've had enough of T.J."

Concern flickered across her face. "Is he blaming you for your father lecturing him?"

"It's just hockey stuff," he said, not wanting to get into it.

Her phone beeped with a text, and she lifted it out of her purse. "Chris is getting impatient. Keep an eye on Jory while I'm gone, okay? He's in his room."

Brad nodded. Once his mother left, he trudged upstairs to visit the only brother he didn't feel like checking from behind and smashing into the boards.

Chapter Nine

T.J. handed his completed test to the history teacher and slid back into his seat while the other students hunched over their papers. They would use every minute until the bell rang. He'd guess his score was somewhere in the mid-to-high seventies. T.J had deliberately skimped on the essay questions.

He hadn't studied for his Forensic Science test tomorrow, figuring his memory would be enough for a B-minus, nor had he put much effort into his paper on the imagist movement that changed English literature.

Once the bell rang, Randy Keller caught up to T.J. in the corridor. "Hey, why did you turn in the test so fast? Aren't you afraid you rushed it?"

T.J.'s natural competitiveness kicked in as he surveyed his classmate, a dark-haired boy with steel-rimmed glasses and a condescending attitude. According to the rumor mill, Randy claimed that "a girl and a hockey player" would never beat him for valedictorian. T.J. could accept Jenna Marcus outperforming him as she never badmouthed anyone, but he had looked forward to knocking Randy off his pedestal.

"I knew all the answers," he said with a shrug, enjoying Randy's stricken expression. Of course, Randy would cheer up after the updated class rankings.

"I knew them too," Randy said. "But it's easy to make a careless mistake. I always double-check my work. I'm surprised you don't."

"Thanks for your concern. See you." T.J. went down the hall to his locker and deposited his books.

Brad was opening the next locker, ignoring him. They both had lunch this period, but since they were barely speaking, walking to the cafeteria together wasn't an option. T.J. closed his locker door, determined to reach their table of friends first and stake out his seat. Not that he felt like listening to Matt and Russ apologize for the fifth time. Matt regretted succumbing to parental pressure and snitching on his teammates, and Russ blamed himself for the whole mess.

"Hey, hockey stars." Peyton Aldrich, a figure skater who T.J. often saw at the rink, sidled over to them in a cropped green sweater and black leggings that hugged her curves. Brad gave her a cool nod. She twirled a lock of her sleek highlights and appraised T.J. "Nice hat trick the other day. You were heating up the ice."

T.J. rested a palm against his locker. "You too. Nice double axel in gym last week." Due to the school's adjacent rink, students could enroll in a skating class for PE. Most kids skated laps and learned basic moves, but Peyton had permission to rehearse her routines—making her the center of attention.

Her sly smile widened. "You were watching me?"

"It's hard not to. You're good."

"I'm good at lots of things."

He didn't miss the sultry note in her voice. T.J. searched for a safe topic. "I hear competitions is one of them. How's that going? Got any coming up?"

"A couple. I came in second last month. Give me your phone so I can send you a video."

After a hesitation, he pulled his cell out of his jeans pocket. She added her number to his contacts and texted herself from his device. When she passed it back, her hand lingered in his for a few seconds. "I'll reply with the video tonight. You'll have to tell me how it's going with the scouts. I'm sure they're fighting over who gets to have you."

Brad shut his locker, loudly, and T.J. remembered he was there. "Hey, Peyton, about the texting. You know I'm going out with Kayla, right?"

"She lets you have friends, doesn't she?" Without waiting for an answer, she continued, "Talk to you later, T.J. Bye, Brad." She flipped back her hair and ambled down the now deserted hall.

Once she was out of earshot, Brad shook his head and broke the twenty-four-hour silence between them. "Dude, you've done some stupid things, but this is one of the stupidest."

"I told her I had a girlfriend. Did you miss that part when you were eavesdropping?"

"That's never stopped her before. I hope you're not planning to mess around with her while you're still seeing Kayla."

"Come on, you know I wouldn't do that," T.J. said.

"So if Peyton texts when you're together, you'll tell Kayla who it is?" Brad waited a beat. "Didn't think so."

He elbowed by T.J. who stuffed the phone into his pocket. He didn't need his brother laying a guilt trip on him. Sure, a fling with Peyton might interest him if he were single, but he wasn't. Not yet. T.J. had been upfront that he was dating someone, and he would never dump Kayla over the holidays. Okay, perhaps he was opening the door a sliver to see what developed with Peyton. But as long as they were just friends until he and Kayla broke up, there was nothing wrong with giving her his number.

Was there?

***

That afternoon before practice, T.J. taped his stick as Trey grilled him for details about Alexis, Kayla's friend. Trey sat on the bench beside him, chomping on cheese curls in between questions. "Did Kayla say anything about the party?" Crunch. "Does Alex like me?"

"I haven't talked to her much." T.J. eyed Brad, standing a couple feet away. "My phone got taken away for the weekend," he added bitterly.

"Better make your move, Trey," Brad quipped. "Soon Kayla won't be giving him inside information. T.J.'s relationships are like milk. They've got an expiration date."

"You don't know what you're talking about. Mind your own business."

"I'll stay out of yours if you stay out of mine." Brad went to retrieve his stick from the rack near the entrance.

"Well, that was awkward," Trey joked, brushing off the orange crumbs dusting his practice jersey. "Sometimes you guys make me glad I'm an only child."

T.J. couldn't fathom what that must be like. When he and his brothers were getting along, it was great. There was always someone around to hang out with and to have his back. But when one of them was annoying him, which happened way too often, then being an only child sounded even better than a luxury private suite at the TD Garden.

"So about Alexis . . ." Trey began.

"Time to hit the ice, boys," Coach Reynolds said, emerging from his office in a winter hat and sweats. His mustache bristled as he observed Trey digging into the cheese curls. "Arenson, how many times have I told you to have a healthy snack before practice?"

Trey raised the crinkled bag. "It is healthy. It's got cheese, Coach. That's in one of the five food groups."

"If it's that nutritious then you should be able to give me fifty push-ups on the ice. Get out there, Arenson." Coach Reynolds walked toward the door with a clipboard tucked under his arm.

"Will everyone else be doing push-ups, Coach?" Trey called after him a trifle nervously.

"Nope," Reynolds replied over his shoulder.

T.J. chuckled. He could always count on Trey for comic relief.

His lighter mood was short-lived. During practice, Brad and Chris kept scuffling over the puck in the corners—elbowing, slashing, and high-sticking each other. They targeted him with their roughing too, but T.J. refused to get provoked. His brothers lacked the same restraint.

"McKendricks, unless you want to spend the rest of practice in the penalty box, tone it down out there!" Coach Reynolds yelled after Chris and Brad almost came to blows.

"What's going on with those two?" Trey muttered to T.J. near the goal crease.

Shrugging, T.J. watched his brothers exchange one last scowl before they skated away from each other. He hadn't noticed them fighting over the weekend, but then again, he'd been holed up in his room last night. T.J. hadn't seen them this morning either. Brad was stuck taking the bus as part of his punishment, and Chris always rode it with his friends. By the time T.J. came downstairs, they had already gone.

As Brad skimmed around the boards, McCann zoomed up behind him and hooked his ankle. Brad sprawled to the ice and Coach Reynolds' whistle shrilled.

"What the hell do you think you're doing?" Brad demanded, rising to his feet. T.J. groaned inwardly.

"What's the matter, embarrassed you tripped?" McCann dropped his stick and shoved Brad.

"All right, you want to go, McCann? Let's do it." Brad tore off his gloves while McCann did the same. They grabbed each other's jersey, and McCann cocked back his arm to throw a punch. Brad pushed against his shoulder, deflecting the force, before launching a punch of his own.

Coach Reynolds yelled from the bench, and T.J. swore. How many times was his twin going to get himself in trouble? In unison, he and Chris veered up to their grappling teammates, squeezing between them and ducking to avoid flying fists. T.J. clamped down on Brad's arms while Chris did the same with McCann.

Once again Coach Reynold's whistle pierced the air. "Break it up, or you're both sitting out the first game of the tournament!" he bellowed.

Cursing under his breath, Brad shook T.J. off him. "You'd better watch it, McCann."

McCann snorted. "I'm terrified."

"Glen, go take a shower and cool off!" Reynolds barked. "Brad, get on the bench. Neither of you leave the rink till I've talked to you."

After practice, once they had showered and changed, a subdued T.J., Trey, and Chris waited on a locker room bench while Brad got rebuked in the coaches' office. McCann had left, having received his lecture earlier.

Once Brad emerged, he halted in front of Chris. "Did you see what your *friend* did? I can't believe you hung out with him yesterday."

This was news to T.J. He'd heard Chris had gone to a movie, but assumed it was with one of his usual friends. That explained the clashing between his brothers on the ice. And why Brad had been so easily goaded by McCann. "That's who you were with?"

"Maybe if you weren't so busy butting into *my* life, you'd know that," Brad retorted.

"You oughta talk," Chris shot back. "You can't tell me who to be friends with."

"Here we go," Trey muttered, his shoulders slouching in resignation.

Frustration rocketing through him, T.J. blew out a long puff of air. He had dealt with enough fighting lately. Soon it would affect his hockey sense, and he wasn't risking that. Not with his college and junior prospects on the line. "I'm done. I'm not cleaning up your messes anymore, Brad. You're running scared, and if you want to sabotage yourself, then go ahead. You're not taking me down with you."

He scrutinized Chris. "I don't buy this friendship crap. You know how McCann is. You've seen how he hates us. He's trying to piss us off, and I'm starting to think you are too. If you've got a problem with Brad and me, then just say it. Stop playing games." T.J. stood and collected his bag, aware that they were all watching him in stunned silence. "If you want a ride, let's go."

T.J. slammed out the door. He'd won this round. And he'd win this tournament and land a college commitment, with or without his brothers' help.

Chapter Ten

Brad tried to shove T.J.'s accusation out of his mind over the next couple days, but it kept invading his thoughts. Was he letting his fears rule him and sabotaging himself? And what was Chris's deal? Brad and T.J. had supported his goal of making varsity. They'd always supported him. Yet, it did seem as if he was deliberately antagonizing them.

Brad and his brothers weren't arguing anymore, but they avoided each other as much as possible. Other than terse communication on the ice, he hadn't talked to them since the locker room blow-up.

On Thursday, even though he wasn't in the Christmas spirit, Brad found himself in a better mood due to the hockey pep rally, early release before school break, and the meeting he'd finally arranged with Sherry. After the pep rally, as enthusiastic students streamed toward the gym doors, he waited for her at the top of the bleachers. The band's performance of *We Will Rock You* by Queen had pumped him up, building Brad's excitement for the tournament.

He had to agree with T.J. on one point. Hockey was what mattered. Not that the other stuff didn't, but when the world went topsy-turvy, he needed to grasp onto something for stability. No matter where he played or at what level, hockey was Brad's anchor as long as he held onto it.

Across from him, banners and posters plastered the walls bearing slogans like *Hockey With Heart*, *Can't Hide Our Bayview*

Pride, and *Fast and Furious*. Brad's favorite highlighted his number: *Have No Fear, #17 Is Here*. Another, which he rolled his eyes at, honored T.J. with the words *Born To Play Hockey #23*. And for Trey, *Behind The Gear Is Someone You Should Fear. Go Trey!*

Sherry climbed the bleachers and sank beside him in a knit sweater emblazoned with a reindeer and candy cane leggings. A light-up ornament necklace hung past the reindeer's red pom pom nose, and dangling Christmas tree earrings swung against her cheeks. Brad inhaled the spicy scent of her gingerbread body spray. She loved the perfume stores at the mall, collecting different fragrances for different seasons.

"You look like one of Santa's elves," Brad said. "A hot elf that distracts all the others from getting any work done."

She eyed the light blue and white hockey jersey tucked into his jeans, the shirt he wore for home games. "You look like a jock. You should be rocking a Santa hat like Trey."

"Trey told me he's also wearing Grinch boxers. That's an image I could've done without."

"Me too. Thanks a lot."

Below them, Student Council members removed posters from the walls and batted around stray balloons. Brad released a deep breath. "Listen. Sorry about the party and for how I treated you. I guess I've been freaked out about all the changes in my life and didn't know how much it bothered me."

Sherry nodded. "I understand that, just not the way you handled it. So, what now?"

"I'll be honest with my girlfriend, for starters. And my parents are making me see a counselor."

"I saw one when I first moved here and was missing my friends. Most of them I knew since kindergarten. Counseling was no big deal. She gave me ideas on how to build my confidence and make new friends. I went for about six months, and then I didn't need it anymore."

Brad wished he'd known Sherry when she arrived in Bayview. It disturbed him to imagine her lonely and homesick. T.J. met her first, and they'd hit it off as they were both new. He encouraged Brad to ask her out, sensing their interest in each other. "I never really thought about how hard it must've been to move. I forget sometimes that you grew up in Florida."

"It was tough at first, but this is home now, too." Sherry reached for his hand and interlaced their fingers. "And now next fall, I'll have to start over again. College will be a huge change even if I'm back in Florida. I'll miss you, my parents, and the friends I've made here. I'm a little freaked out, too."

"You shouldn't be. You'll do great."

"So will you. I'm sure of it. Look, about what happened at Russ's house . . . *that's* the kind of thing that would make us drift apart. When I call to hear your voice, I want to talk to my boyfriend, not the insensitive guy I saw last weekend."

"That's who you'll get. I promise."

"In that case, let's pretend there's a mistletoe above us." She raised her head for a kiss, and Brad merged his mouth with hers. A swell of emotions rushed through him, the usual sizzle from kissing Sherry along with relief that he hadn't destroyed their relationship.

When they pulled apart, Brad fumbled into his backpack on the bench beside him. He drew out a small box wrapped in snowman-patterned paper. "I have something for you."

"Oh no, I left your present at my house. I forgot that you're grounded."

"Don't worry about it. I wanted you to have this before Christmas."

Flashing him a smile, she tore off the paper and opened a velvet box. Sherry gasped at the sterling silver bracelet adorned with blue and silver glass beads and snowflake charms. "It's beautiful! I love it."

Brad's mom had helped him pick it out a few weeks earlier. He'd thought it fit Sherry's taste, but buying jewelry wasn't his strong point so he'd appreciated the second opinion. "I'm glad."

She slipped the bracelet around her wrist and leaned in for another kiss. A few catcalls from her friends made them reluctantly separate. "I guess our vice president's too busy to help us clean up," one girl teased.

Brad grinned, noting the blush painting Sherry's cheeks. "I'd better go find a ride. T.J.'s probably long gone."

Since they didn't have practice today, the players could leave at dismissal. Brad forgot to tell his brother he'd be running late. As part of being grounded, he rode the bus to school. His mother let him drive home from the rink with T.J. and Chris if they didn't go anywhere else. That wasn't an issue since the brothers hardly spoke unless Trey or another teammate accompanied them. Otherwise, music filled the silence.

"Maybe not. He asked me in History if I'd talked to you. I told him we were meeting after the pep rally, and he said to go easy on you."

"He did?"

"Yeah." A flicker of amusement passed over her face. "He said you might act like an idiot, but that you really care about me."

"Of course he had to throw in the idiot comment," Brad said. "But he's right. About both things."

"Well, I'm glad you're *my* idiot. Merry Christmas, Brad." Sherry pressed another kiss on his cheek, and marched down the steps to join her fellow Student Council members on the gym floor. Brad smiled as one of her friends lifted her arm and admired the bracelet.

Once outside, Brad scanned the senior lot for T.J.'s car. He spotted his twin shooting hoops at the nearby basketball court. Despite the chilly air, T.J.'s letter jacket lay on the pavement. He must have been playing a while. Brad halted on the foul line. "Thanks for waiting. Where's Chris?"

"He took the bus. Didn't feel like hanging around."

Brad held out his hands, signaling for his brother to toss him the ball. T.J. passed it to him, and Brad aimed. After the ball struck the rim, T.J. caught it on the bounce.

"How'd it go with Sherry? Hope it went better than that pathetic shot."

"I'm just getting warmed up, loser. It was fine." Brad watched his twin land a jump shot. "I heard you were rooting for us to get back together. Since when?"

T.J. threw the ball to him. "Since I realized you're less of an ass when you're with her than when you're not." He cracked a sheepish grin. "And since it was none of my business, anyway."

"You might've been off-base about Sherry and me, but you had a point about everything else. I have been running scared." Brad aimed again and made the basket. "It's just a lot of big changes coming up, you know?"

"Yeah. It's been stressful for me too."

"What's the deal with Kayla? Why are you thinking about breaking up with her?" Brad kept his voice neutral. "It seems like she gives you enough space."

With a sigh, T.J. recovered the ball and raked a hand through his sweaty hair. "She invited me for Christmas Eve and to a wedding in February."

By the grim tone, Brad would've thought his brother was getting sidelined from the state tournament with a ruptured Achilles tendon. "What's wrong with that?"

"It's a sign that she's getting too serious. I don't need a girl getting possessive."

"How is that possessive? Did you want her to ask some other guy to the wedding?"

"No," T.J. admitted, the ball still tucked under his arm.

"Sometimes I think you're a little paranoid. That last girl you dated sent a million texts, but not all of them have been that bad. None were as great as Kayla though. If you like her, don't screw this up."

T.J. remained quiet, and Brad plunged ahead. "Who else is going tomorrow? Is it just a family thing?"

"Some of their friends and neighbors are coming. It's an open house."

"Then that's nothing. Stop by for an hour and give her your present. It'll give you an excuse to leave all the fun at Dad's. You got her something, right?"

"Yeah, a Red Sox T-shirt. She mentioned she wanted one."

"I would've gone with jewelry, but whatever. You're reading way too much into these invites."

T.J. dribbled the ball a few times, staring down at the pavement, and then glanced up. "Thanks for putting it in perspective. I don't know why I panicked."

"You haven't had the best example to follow. Watching Mom and Dad's relationship go downhill has messed up both of us." As Brad spoke the words aloud, he saw the truth behind them. Their parents' marriage had affected him and T.J. in different ways, but with equally damaging results. T.J. feared commitment or anything that resembled it.

And I'm afraid of things not working out. Of being alone.

"Yeah, maybe," T.J. said. "I'll tell her I can come over tomorrow."

"For the wedding though, she'd be better off with a date who can dance."

"You're hilarious." T.J's phone chimed with a text. He passed the basketball to Brad, checked his cell, and groaned.

"Peyton?" She was hot and a talented figure skater, but high-maintenance and stirred up drama. Brad was glad his brother chose Kayla.

"No, I haven't responded much, so I think she got the hint. She was all over Matt this morning. It's Dad. He saw my grades on the parent portal."

"You got an A, and he wanted an A-plus?" Brad asked, dribbling a few times.

"Try two B-minuses and a C-plus."

"Really? Are your classes tougher this year?" Three mediocre grades seemed unusual for his brother.

"Not exactly. Dad's always pressuring me about being the valedictorian, so I'm taking myself out of the running."

"I thought you wanted to be valedictorian." T.J. was just as competitive with his grades as he was with hockey. It wasn't like him to blow a chance at being number one.

"I don't want to give him the satisfaction." T.J. shook his head. "You know what's crazy? I doubt he even checked your grades on the portal."

"He used to when I was getting Ds. Then I'd hear about it. Dad congratulated me the first time I made the honor roll, but now he doesn't say anything. He thinks I've reached my full potential."

Dad acted the same way with Chris, whose grades mirrored Brad's. School came harder to them and they got more easily distracted. Jory, though, was like T.J., always at the top of his class. He'd be the next boy wonder. Brad hoped his youngest brother could handle the pressure.

"Well, I've definitely reached mine," T.J. said. "At least with my GPA."

"Only because you're holding yourself back from your goal. Aren't you also hurting yourself? "

"The only goals that matter right now are in hockey. Come on." T.J. strode over to his car and dumped the basketball into the trunk.

When they got home, their mother and Jory were baking in the kitchen with trays and plastic containers spread out on the granite counter and *Rockin' Around the Christmas Tree* blasting from Mom's cell phone. The buttery vanilla scent of fresh sugar cookies wafted through the air. Brad snatched a Santa hat off the tray right after Jory sprinkled on the red sugar.

"Give me one of those," T.J. said, scooping up a tree smeared with green frosting.

"Stop snacking on cookies," Mom warned Jory, who was biting into a snowman. Patches of flour smattered her velvety black sweatshirt, emblazoned with a wreath. "Your father's taking you out to eat later."

"He is?" Brad asked. "I thought we weren't seeing him till tomorrow."

"I need to finish my Christmas shopping," Jory answered. "He's taking me to the mall."

"The mall the day before Christmas Eve? Are you crazy?"

"I'm going to lift weights." T.J.'s abrupt comment didn't surprise Brad. He was disappearing before Dad showed up. "You coming?"

"In a few minutes." If Brad had to suffer through another dysfunctional family holiday, then he was at least savoring the cookies. With his brothers' appetites, they wouldn't last long.

T.J.'s cell rang as he left the kitchen. Brad poured himself some milk and sat down next to Chris, who shot him a sideways glance. "You guys are working out together? What're you, friends again?"

"Why not? It's the season of brotherly love and all that crap. Want to lift weights with us?"

"I guess so. It's not like I've got anything better to do." Chris shrugged, and Brad hoped this was the start of things going back to normal between them. He'd always been close to Chris, but lately they fought all the time.

Their mother carried over a festive container of chocolate walnut fudge. "One of my patients made this for me. Anyone want a piece?"

"Sure," Brad said.

He, Chris, and Jory had each downed several slices of fudge when T.J. returned. "Brad!"

His twin brother's voice sounded different, higher in pitch. Brad sipped his milk and asked, "What's up?"

T.J.'s green eyes gleamed with a spark Brad hadn't seen since the team made it into the state finals. "That was Coach O'Reilly at BC," he said, referring to the assistant coach who had attended their season opener. "He left you a message on your cell phone. They're . . . they're offering us a verbal commitment to play in two years." His voice thickened with emotion.

Brad's heart slammed in his chest. Could it be true? BC wanted them enough to make an offer in high school? Slowly, he rose to his feet. "Are you serious?"

Grinning, T.J. nodded. "We did it, bro. We're going to BC!"

Their mother shrieked and flew over to embrace T.J. "Oh my God, both of you? That's great!"

"Cool!" Jory exclaimed. "Congrats."

Brad struggled to comprehend what was happening. Two years. That meant the coaches still wanted them to develop in a junior league. "What about junior?"

"Coach O'Reilly has been talking us up to the staff of the Youngstown team in Ohio. He said someone will be in touch. He sounded confident they'll draft us."

Relief swept over Brad. Scoring a D1 commitment this early and having an inside track with a USHL team would ease so much pressure. And somehow leaving home and playing junior seemed less intimidating with T.J. by his side. He tried to focus as T.J. recapped the details of his conversation.

"I'm so happy for you guys. You've worked so hard for this." Their mother drew Brad into a bear hug. Chris exited the kitchen, mumbling that he was going down the street to his friend Jaden's house. He hadn't said one word about the news. Brad's kid brother was getting moodier by the day.

"I told the coach you'd call him back," T.J. said.

"How about it, Mom?" Brad asked as he and his mother separated. "Can I get out of technology jail to call the coach and Sherry?"

She laughed. "For a few minutes. Your cell's on my dresser if you want to listen to the message."

On his way out of the room, Brad exchanged high fives with his brothers. Behind him, he heard them doing a Google search, estimating the travel distance to Ohio. Jory didn't like the sound of a twelve-hour drive, but it appeased him that the flight was less than two hours.

Brad went upstairs to retrieve his cell, a lightness in his step. He didn't even mind the strains of *Jingle Bells* that drifted from Mom's phone. Santa had delivered one special gift.

Chapter Eleven

For once, T.J. couldn't wait to see his father. He stood in the kitchen with Jory and Mom, barely able to contain his grin. He paced to the window and glanced out at the empty driveway. No sign of Dad yet, but he should be here for Jory soon.

T.J.'s heartbeat drummed in his chest. He was going to wear the maroon and gold of the Boston College Eagles! Sell-out crowds of eight thousand fans would fill the Conte Forum, known as Kelley Rink for hockey games, and watch him play. T.J. had read up on the school's rich hockey history, learning how the ice rink was named for longtime BC hockey coach John "Snooks" Kelley, who coached the Eagles for thirty-six years and was the first NCAA coach to win 500 games.

Now he and Brad would become part of that legacy. They'd even get to play in the Beanpot Hockey Tournament, which invited the four major hockey programs in Boston—Boston College, Boston University, Northeastern, and Harvard—to face off in a two-game series at the TD Garden.

T.J. loved everything about the tour, especially the state-of-the-art men's hockey locker room with the BC logo adorning a wall that resembled the stonework on the historic buildings around campus. The logo was everywhere, even splashed across the ceiling, reminding T.J. that this was the big time.

Everything was high tech, like the players' stalls in the main team rooms with their backlit nameplates and LED lights around the footlocker portion. All the stalls had individual ventilation systems and fans to dry the hockey equipment. A senior NHL draft pick showed them the stick rooms, saunas, Smart Board teaching stations for game film analysis and strategizing, and televisions and ping-pong tables for relaxing. It would be quite an upgrade from the Bayview locker room.

After another peek out the window, T.J. reclaimed his seat at the table. Finally, he would satisfy his father, even make him proud. How could Dad find fault with Boston College? T.J. remembered reading that the school only had a 29 percent acceptance rate. They'd both get what they wanted.

And Mom and Dad can stop fighting over me.

Brad came back downstairs as their father's Cadillac was pulling into the driveway. "I texted him to come inside. Is that okay, Mom?"

She cleared her throat. "Of course. You have amazing news to share. Why don't you guys go talk to him in the living room? Jory, help me clean up this mess." Their mother covered the remaining frosting with a layer of plastic wrap and gestured for Jory to put away the flour and sugar.

T.J. opened the front door for their father. Dad stepped inside, wearing his long black overcoat. "Hello, boys. You had something to tell me, Brad? Is everything okay?"

"It's great, actually." Brad leaned against the arm of the couch. Behind him, the red blanket under the Christmas tree displayed several new presents. "You want to tell him, Teej?"

T.J. wondered if their father sensed the excitement crackling in the air. "We both got an offer from BC to play hockey. It's for two years from now. A two-for-four scholarship." That meant they would receive athletic financial aid for two out of four years. "They're recommending us to a USHL team in Ohio."

"Really?" Dad's brows furrowed and then released. "BC is having you sign a letter of intent?"

"Not yet, it's way too early for that," T.J. said. "A letter of intent applies to the upcoming academic year."

T.J. could recite most of the information on the National Letter of Intent website. The letter was an official binding agreement between a prospective student-athlete and a member school, with the student committing to attend the institution full-time for one academic year in exchange for athletic financial aid.

Their father frowned. "This is just a verbal commitment?"

Just? So far, Dad wasn't reacting as he'd hoped. T.J. should have expected the skepticism. A verbal commitment was an oral contract between the athlete and the coach that could be announced anytime. Athletes typically shared it on social media. Until the boys signed a letter of intent, the agreement was unofficial.

"A verbal commitment from BC means a lot, Dad," Brad interjected.

"It's *non-binding*." Dad scrubbed his hands over his face. "A coach can retract the offer or change it at any point. Have you accepted it yet?"

"He gave us a week, but we're going to," Brad said. "Then we'll confirm the conversation over email so it's documented. Don't worry, Dad. We know what we're doing."

"An email doesn't make it binding." Their father walked a couple feet. "I understand you accepting these terms, Brad. I don't think you have anything to lose." Missing Brad's grimace, he fixed his gaze on T.J. "But for you, it's a risk. What if there's a coaching change, or they recruit more players than they need? What if you get injured or have a slump? If they don't honor the offer, then you'll have wasted two years."

Anger boiled inside T.J., blood flow surging to his face. He fought to keep his emotions at bay as he closed the space between him and his father. "Can't you ever support me? This is what I've been working toward. This is huge, but all you can do is criticize."

"I'm trying to keep you from making a big mistake," Dad retorted. "Judging by your grades, you've gotten distracted and ruined your chances for valedictorian. All you're thinking about is hockey, and they're not even giving you a four-year-scholarship."

"Dad, D1 hockey coaches only get eighteen full scholarships and usually divide them into partials," Brad said, leaning forward. "You're not being realistic. T.J. will get academic scholarships too, and once we've gone there a couple years, the athletic aid might get extended. We couldn't be in a better position."

T.J. chuckled without humor. "Come on, do you really think he'll listen to you? You're the dumb jock, remember? At least according to Dad."

"What's he talking about?" their father asked, glancing from one to the other.

Brad nailed T.J. with a "thanks a lot" glare before focusing on their father. "I'm glad you're not fighting me on hockey, but you treat me like that's all I've got going for me. I've pulled up my grades, and I've been doing writing and video production. But you never ask about anything besides hockey."

Dad regarded him for a moment and then answered, "I think you have lots of potential, Brad, but it was difficult persuading you to take your grades seriously. Nothing I said ever motivated you to study. It wasn't until you became intent on playing college hockey that you applied yourself. Once you improved your marks, I didn't want to push you too hard. I thought if I did, it might turn you off. Sometimes you can be rebellious."

Their father clamped a hand on Brad's shoulder. "I'm sorry if I gave you the wrong idea. If it's okay, I'd like to see some of your writing and video projects."

After a few seconds, Brad nodded. "I get what you're saying. Maybe this week I can show you what I've been working on."

"I'd like that," Dad said, patting his shoulder one more time.

T.J. watched their father-son bonding moment in disbelief. He didn't want to push *Brad* too hard? Dad didn't want to turn *him* off? So, basically Brad was getting rewarded for being rebellious.

He snorted, unable to hold back any longer. "You don't care about pushing me too hard. No matter how high my GPA is, it's never good enough. I put myself under enough pressure and don't need you breathing down my neck. It's my life, Dad, and I'm done with you controlling it. Just leave me alone!" T.J. was yelling, and his father was gaping, but he didn't care. His pulse hammered, and heat flushed through his body. He'd shouted at his parents before, but had never screamed at either of them like this.

"Hey, T.J.," Brad began, stepping toward him, concern on his face.

"Stay out of it," T.J. snapped, shoving past him. "You don't understand."

Mom entered the room and pinned a furious gaze on their father. "You couldn't just be happy for him. You have to control things. What is the matter with you?"

"Barbara, this is between my son and me," Dad said impatiently. "Give us a chance to work it out."

"You've had plenty of chances and you never listen! Why should this time be any different?" She folded her arms across her chest.

Here they go again. Getting them to stop arguing over him wasn't going to happen. No scholarship would change the fact that T.J.'s parents couldn't stand each other, and that he was the detonator to trigger their explosions.

"Stop it!" Jory yelled from the doorway, his eyes bright with unshed tears. "You're always fighting! I can't take it anymore."

They all spun toward him. Their mother started to speak, but Jory wasn't finished yet. "I'll quit hockey, okay?" His voice trembled. "Dad, you don't have to take me to games and practices anymore, so you can stop arguing about it."

"Jor, that's not why they're arguing," T.J. said.

"Well, they have before. Dad says our whole weekend revolves around my games, and Mom says she's driven us around on weekends for years and that it's about time he took some turns." Jory sniffed and shot an apprehensive look at his parents. "I know you're splitting up because of me."

"Trust me, they fight about me a lot more than you," T.J. said.

As he watched his younger brother, realization descended over him. *I'm just like a ten-year-old, blaming myself for my parents' divorce.* Jory wasn't to blame for their parents' train wreck of a marriage. Neither was T.J. Arguments over his future and Jory's schedule were symptoms of a much bigger problem. Dad acting controlling was nothing new, but Mom didn't take it like she used to when T.J. was younger. It was as if she could no longer contain her resentment. Maybe his parents didn't know how to talk with each other and resolve their conflicts—and gave up trying because there was nothing left to salvage.

"Boys, none of this is your fault." All the anger had left Mom's voice, a note of sadness replacing it.

Their father spoke, his expression unreadable. "I don't want you to give up hockey, Jory. I shouldn't have said that. Sometimes I get fatigued and grouchy, and that makes me say things I don't mean."

"It sounded like you meant it." Jory stared him down the same way he faced the opposing center during games.

T.J.'s phone alerted him to a text, and he slid it out of his jeans. Chris had written: *At McCann's. Bad scene. Can u pick me up?*

Since when was he with McCann? Chris had told them he was going down the street. T.J. tapped back: *What's the address?* He walked over to the coat hook and grabbed his Bayview High jacket. At least rescuing Chris would get him out of here. His cell sounded again with his brother sharing a street address on the other side of town.

"Where are you going?" his mother asked.

T.J. sighed. He didn't want to get Chris in trouble, but after the party incident, he'd rather not risk getting grounded again. Besides, his parents needed to wake up and see what was going on with their own kids. "Chris needs a ride from McCann's house."

"McCann?" Brad asked sharply, striding over and snatching T.J.'s phone. "What's he doing there? Bad scene? What the hell does that mean?"

"I thought he was staying in the neighborhood. He told me he was going to Jayden's. How did he even get there?" Mom twisted a clump of her hair, her face harried.

"McCann must've given him a ride." T.J. flung on his jacket and lifted his keys out of his pocket.

"Can I go with T.J.?" Brad asked.

To T.J.'s surprise, Dad nodded. "Come right back. Remember, you're still grounded. And Thomas . . . thanks for going to get him."

Not responding, T.J. opened the door, grateful to escape.

***

Fifteen minutes later, T.J. pulled up in front of a hulking apartment building with peeling gray paint and a dirt parking lot. Chris sat on the cracked front steps in a hooded sweatshirt and jeans. He stood when he saw the car and opened the back door.

"Thanks," he mumbled, sliding in.

"What's going on in there?" Brad glared at the building. T.J. drove toward the exit before Brad bolted inside to pulverize their teammate.

"McCann had some loser friends over, and they were drinking and smoking pot," Chris said, fastening his seatbelt. "A couple were taking pills. I don't know what they were. McCann offered to drive me home, but he was stoned, so I told him I already had a ride."

Brad hit the glove compartment with his fist. "Why do you hang around with him? You're not dumb, Chris. You've got to know that he's bad news."

Silence.

"Answer the question," T.J. ordered, turning onto the main

road. "We came to pick you up, so you owe us that much."

"Fine. You and Brad are always busy, and all you talk about is playing junior and getting into college. I figured hanging around with McCann would get your attention." Chris hesitated. "He's not as bad as you think though. His family's way more messed up than ours. I'll bet that has a lot to do with how he acts."

That didn't surprise T.J. McCann's father jeered the officials and coaches at games and reprimanded his son for missed shots. Still, that didn't justify McCann's attitude. You either rose above adversity or let it dictate your life.

"Why didn't you tell us you were feeling left out?" Brad asked.

"What's the point? You'll be gone next year, anyway." Chris scoffed. "Where are you going? Ohio? That's not exactly around the corner."

"It's not Switzerland either," T.J. said. "Besides, you're glued to your phone, so you can text or call whenever you want, and it's not like we're never coming home."

"We should be in Massachusetts for your senior year, so don't get any ideas about my room," Brad warned. "I'll still need it sometimes."

"It won't be the same. Mostly, it'll be just me, Mom, and Jory." Chris was quiet for a moment. "Mom and Dad might date other people. They could even get remarried. To someone with kids. You won't have to deal with any of that."

"Sure we will," T.J. said, hooking a right onto Main Street. "There will be times we're living at home, and even when we're away, it'll still affect us. But there's no sense worrying about it. They might never get remarried, or it could be when you're out of school."

"Listen, Chris, you're not the only one anxious about the future," Brad said. "Next year, I've got to move into a house with strangers, prove myself to new coaches and teammates, and think about all the guys Sherry's meeting in Florida. Then for college, everything will change again."

"Is that why you got drunk that night?"

"Yeah. The pressure got to me. I'm glad you were smarter than I was and didn't let McCann's crowd talk you into anything stupid."

"Your hangover had a lot to do with it," Chris admitted. "That looked like it really sucked. Can you guys try to live together next year? Do those families ever take two players?"

T.J. hadn't considered that idea and wasn't sure how he felt about it. It might be nice to have his brother in the same house, but then again, that could be too much togetherness.

"I don't know. Since we're talking about fears, one of mine is Brad and I killing each other," T.J. joked, concentrating on the road again.

"Same. That's asking a lot for one family to take two McKendricks," Brad agreed.

"Especially lately. You got grounded for sneaking in drunk. Chris is about to get grounded for sneaking out."

"I am?" With a groan, Chris sank back in his seat.

Brad laughed, and Chris said, "Glad you're so amused."

"It's not that. I was just thinking about how T.J.'s big rebellion was getting Bs."

"B-minuses, and there was a C-plus too," T.J. said defensively.

"Yeah, and it's bugging you, isn't it?" Brad countered.

It really was. T.J. hated having his GPA blemished. If those grades reflected his best effort, that would be different, but he could have performed much better.

"Wow, Teej. Next you're gonna be showing up for school five minutes late." Chris snickered.

"Come on, you're not letting Randy Keller beat you for valedictorian, are you?" Brad asked. "Don't let your stubbornness blow this. You know what Coach Reynolds says. You miss one hundred percent of the shots you don't take."

Their coach had a poster of the Wayne Gretzky quote hanging in his office. T.J. tightened his grip around the steering wheel.

Brad was right. He'd regret not taking this shot.

No more caring about his father's reactions. As long as T.J. believed he was making the right decisions, that was all that mattered. Even without Dad's support, he could still count on his mother, brothers, and friends. Kayla would be ecstatic about the BC offer. T.J. decided to drop off Brad and Chris at home and tell her the news in person. They'd been dating a while now, and she deserved a boyfriend who didn't push her away.

He turned onto the street that led to their neighborhood. "I'll see if I can do some extra credit and get back on track. It might be too late for valedictorian, but I'd settle for salutatorian. That won't be good enough for Dad, but so what?"

"Maybe you should give him another chance," Brad said. "Find out if he was affected by anything you told him. You heard him with Jory and me. It seemed like he was listening for once."

"The key word is 'seemed.' You're not seriously showing him your fiction, are you? You're just asking for criticism. Nothing's good enough for him."

"I'll start with some articles and videos. I can't imagine giving him anything else, not right now. But I wouldn't mind getting to that point someday." Brad shrugged. "We'll see what happens."

"I think you're getting carried away by his little speech, but do what you want."

"What did I miss, anyway?" Chris demanded.

While Brad filled him in on the latest turmoil, T.J. let them off in the driveway. His father's car was gone. Had Dad and Jory kept their shopping plans?

Dismissing family from his mind, T.J. drove to Kayla's where he spent the next few hours helping her younger sister decorate a gingerbread house, watching the movie *Elf*, and sampling treats for tomorrow. As he'd expected, Kayla congratulated him and shared the news with her enthusiastic parents who peppered him with questions. She hugged T.J. when he mentioned that he could visit on Christmas Eve after all and that he was available for the wedding. By the time he entered his house, his mood had improved, and it even felt like Christmas.

When he got upstairs, T.J. stopped in Jory's room. "Hey, little brother. You okay?" he asked from the doorway.

Jory glanced up from the bean bag chair and lowered his Mike Lupica sports book to his side. "Yeah. You?"

T.J. nodded. "I hung out at Kayla's for a while. Put piping and gumdrops on a gingerbread house. Don't tell anyone."

"Did you at least get to eat it?" Jory grinned.

"Are you kidding? No way. It's a work of art. Did you go to the mall?"

"Yeah. Dad left a present on your bed. He wants you to open it."

Their father had gotten him a gift? Why give it to him now and not Christmas Eve? His curiosity ignited, T.J. asked, "He bought it tonight?"

"Yeah, we went all over the place searching for one. Mom gave him the idea."

T.J. retreated to his room, skeptical to see the peace offering. He found a rectangular package on his bed, wrapped in paper from his mother's collection. Wow, they really had teamed up on this. Santa on the roof in goalie pads would have been less shocking. T.J. read the attached note. *Let's talk this week. Dad.* Since when did his father talk without chastising?

He ripped off the paper, opened the box, and drew out a maroon sweatshirt emblazoned in gold with Boston College and the BC Eagles logo. He sat on his bed, gazing at the gift in his lap.

What the hell did this mean? Obviously, Dad was implying that he'd accepted the decision. And for Mom to help, she must believe him. But T.J. wasn't convinced.

What if this was a Band-Aid to get them through the holidays? What if his father was planning a counterargument? Dad could pressure him to enroll for the fall and try to walk on the team, which they both knew would be a wasted effort. If the coaches wanted him next year, then he'd be signing a letter of intent.

T.J. fingered the BC emblem in the middle of the shirt. His father wasn't like McCann's, who ridiculed him in front of his teammates and spectators. Dad was tough to get along with, but T.J. didn't doubt his father's love for him. He interfered because he wanted the best for T.J.

If he and Brad could put aside their differences and lead their team to the state finals last March, there was hope for him and his father. T.J. never would have expected to bond with his twin after years of sibling rivalry. Now here they were, preparing to spend the next six seasons together. Voluntarily.

He had to trust that this was a genuine effort and that his father wanted to save their deteriorating relationship. He had to trust his dad.

T.J. composed a brief text on his cell. *Thanks for the sweatshirt. See you tomorrow.* A few seconds later, three dots appeared, indicating his father was typing. Looking forward to it. With a slight smile, T.J. pocketed his phone. Brad's words echoed back to him.

You miss one hundred percent of the shots you don't take.

Chapter Twelve

The Bayview Jets skated laps around their half of the home ice while the warm-up clock counted down to the buzzer. They'd made it to the finals of the Christmas tournament, a four-day event showcasing eight teams including their opponent, the Windsor Knights. Brad always liked the annual tournament as it reunited him with old friends from youth programs and camps, so it was a mix of competition and camaraderie. He skated around the net and lingered when he heard Trey conversing with the goal posts.

"Come on, guys, be good to me tonight," Trey muttered, hitting the posts and the crossbar with his stick. "You can do it."

Brad halted in front of him. "Are they saying anything back?"

"Very funny. It's my new ritual."

Trey already tapped the wall with his stick before venturing out on the ice, patted the goalposts whenever the puck dinged the sides and they "made the save," and would drink exactly five sips of a fruit punch-flavored sports drink during intermissions.

"You goalies are nuts," Brad said, shaking his head before taking off.

"You won't say that when I get a shutout," Trey called after him.

Brad didn't know if Trey's talking to the goalposts had any effect, but by the end of the first period, the score was 2-0 Bayview. Brad had scored with a slapshot from the blue line, the puck finding an opening in the top right-hand corner. Later, T.J. netted a wraparound goal, doubling the lead.

A few minutes into the second period, the brothers raced forward on a two-on-two. Brad swerved wide. T.J. faked going wide and cut inside, splitting the defense. He dashed toward the net, his stick slashing back and forth on the ice, while the defensemen hacked at him. T.J. shot low to the left, the puck sailing over the goaltender's glove. Their teammates swarmed around him.

After that goal, everything fell apart and the rest of the second period was a disaster. Matt sent a blind pass to one of Windsor's defensemen, who drilled a wrist shot past Trey. T.J. got called for holding, and the Knights scored a power-play goal. A Windsor forward knocked away a clearing attempt by the right circle and rifled another shot into the net. McCann overskated the puck, and Russ tripped over the blue line.

"We're playing like we've never seen ice before," Brad complained between periods. "We've got to pull it together." He locked eyes with the desolate seniors gathered in front of the bench, even McCann, who he'd wanted to punch all week. Since his parents weren't allowing Chris to hang out with McCann outside of practice, Brad controlled his temper, saving his aggression for the series. "Come on, guys, this is our last Christmas tournament."

"Let's do this," T.J. said.

"On three, give me a 'Jets'," Trey interjected. "One, two, three—Jets!"

Bayview fans cheered when the home team set up for the opening face-off. Brad located Jory standing and clapping beside their father, who was seated but watching the action, for once not tied to his laptop. He'd spotted his mother with a pack of other hockey moms, and Sherry, Kayla, and Trey's new girlfriend Alexis waving handmade signs in the middle of the bleachers.

With two minutes left in regulation, the score still tied 3-3, Coach Reynold rearranged the lines and put Chris out on left wing with T.J. and Brad. *Good move*, Brad thought. Chris had done well on the third line, keeping the puck in the offensive zone and launching several shots on goal.

"Let me see some McKendrick magic out there!" Reynolds shouted.

Adrenaline coursed through Brad. He and his brothers could win this game. After a tumultuous December, they were back in tune with each other. Brad felt the energy, and his coach was gambling on it. They were overcoming their challenges and revved to tackle the new year head-on.

Time to show the world that the McKendricks were unstoppable.

T.J. took the draw, his brothers on either side. The puck squirted loose, and Brad caught it on his stick. He stickhandled along the boards in the Windsor zone. Two defensemen barreled toward him from both sides, edging him into the glass. He slid the puck to T.J. just as a big winger veered onto his twin's tail.

"Pass!" Chris called.

His reaction instant, T.J. spun around and directed the puck toward Chris.

Chris descended on the goaltender alone. He feigned to his forehand. As the goaltender dove, Chris shifted the disk to his backhand and flipped it into the net. The light flashed on, and the crowd exploded.

Dazed from his first varsity goal, Chris stared at the puck, and Brad made a mental note to fetch it for him later. A stream of teammates poured around Chris. Trey raced out of the crease, pumping his arm at his side.

"You did it!" Brad shouted, grabbing his younger brother's shoulders.

"Nice one, bro!" T.J. slapped Chris a high five.

"Nice assist!" Chris accepted more congratulations and then the teams set up for the face-off.

Forty seconds remained. T.J. won the draw and tapped it to Chris, giving Windsor no chance to pull the goalie. The three McKendricks sprinted into the Windsor zone, taking turns passing and firing shots on goal until the buzzer clanged, sending the Bayview fans into a frenzy.

Brad glanced up into the stands, his gaze landing on his father, who miraculously had jumped up along with a beaming Jory. Things are going to be okay. Different, but okay.

He went in search of the puck, pausing to celebrate with his teammates and greet a couple friends from the Windsor Knights. Once Brad retrieved it, he skated back and offered it to Chris.

"Thanks, Brad." Chris grinned at him, his face lit brighter than the scoreboard.

Brad clapped him on the shoulder. Once the season ended—hopefully with a state title—the seniors would leave their team in good hands. As usual, his twin brother read his mind.

T.J. raised his stick in victory. "The torch has been passed."

The End

Thank you for taking the time to read *Offsides*. If you enjoyed this book, please consider telling your friends and teammates, sharing the book on social media, and posting a short review on retail sites. Even a review of one or two lines is a big help. Word of mouth is an author's best friend and much appreciated.

Thank you!

About the Author

Stacy Drumtra wrote her first novel, *Face-Off,* when she was 16 years old and hasn't stopped writing since. Now she is mostly known by her married name, Stacy Juba. She is also the author of the young adult paranormal thriller *Dark Before Dawn,* the children's picture books *The Flag Keeper* and the *Teddy Bear Town Children's E-Book Bundle*, and the adult mystery novels *Twenty-Five Years Ago Today* and *Sink or Swim*. Most recently, she is the author of the Storybook Valley romantic comedy series for adults, which includes titles *Fooling Around With Cinderella* and *Prancing Around With Sleeping Beauty.*

Visit www.stacyjuba.com and sign up for her newsletter to be informed about new releases.

Acknowledgements

This was one of the strangest, most rewarding, projects I've ever undertaken as I had such a unique collaborator—my teenage self.

My first novel, *Face-Off*, was published in the 1990s when I was eighteen. I wrote it during study halls when I was sixteen and entered it in a contest for teenager writers. To my shock, it won and received a contract from a major New York publisher. Once the book came out, the fan mail started arriving. I received letters like this:

"I loved it because I love hockey. The story kind of relates to my family because I have a twin and two younger brothers . . . can you please make a sequel?"

- Matthew from Vermont

"Face-Off was a great book. The reason I picked it out was because it was about hockey. I think that there should be a sequel to it."

- Wesley from Maine

"I would really enjoy another one of your books. The book you wrote was the first book I ever sat down and read the whole thing. I don't read much, but this time I did."

- Richard from Missouri

"This is, by far, one of the best books I have ever read. Face-Off has an excellent climax and a superb plot . . . This is one book I think every hockey fan should read. Your book shows how in hockey, it's not a one-man show and it takes a whole team to win.

I know a sequel to Face-Off would be great. I couldn't change any part of this story to make it better if I tried."

- Adam from Ohio

So, in 1993, I decided to write a sequel. I finished the first draft of *Offsides* when I was twenty, a college sophomore. But when I submitted it to the publisher, there had been a major restructuring and my editor was gone. No one there remembered *Face-Off* as I got rejected with a form letter. Then I sent the story to other publishers. They weren't interested in a sequel to a novel published by another company. Since no one would publish it, I put the book in a drawer.

Fast forward to 2011. After years of working as a reporter and continuing to write fiction, I was back in the publishing game with two adult mystery novels and my young adult supernatural thriller *Dark Before Dawn*. Thanks to the growth of ebooks, there were many more opportunities for authors than there had been in the 1990s.

After a Google search on *Face-Off*, I learned that the Hockey Hall of Fame Junior Education Program had placed the book on its recommended reading list and that *Face-Off* had also been included in *Best Books for Young Teen Readers Grades 7-10*. Wow! A mother even tracked me down at my former place of employment, calling the office and asking if a sequel had been published. Although *Face-Off* was long out-of-print, it wasn't forgotten, at least by the readers.

Since *Face-Off* was only available from used bookstores, I self-published a second edition. It immediately started selling, and I vowed to publish *Offsides* also. I hired a company to scan my old manuscript into a computer so I could work with it again. It had been typed on a word processor and I didn't have access to a digital version. Unfortunately, the scanning process riddled it with formatting errors and odd symbols. Once I corrected the hundreds of mistakes, I realized the manuscript was still a mess.

It was outdated and unrealistic. The route to college hockey is much different today, and the book needed a massive overhaul. My writing skills are also much stronger now, and the lack of character development and description made me cringe!

I began researching junior hockey and Division 1 scholarships, but a family health crisis in 2013 hit me hard, and I stopped writing. When the words finally started flowing again, my muse was directing me to write my romantic comedy series for adults. I needed to write something light and funny. And frankly, *Offsides* still scared me. It really was a mess!

But I couldn't stop thinking about my old friends Brad, T.J., Chris, and Jory, especially since mothers and grandmothers kept emailing me to ask about a sequel. Suddenly, I was inspired to go back to it before another generation outgrew the book.

I listened to the *Face-Off* audiobook narrated by the fantastic Maxwell Glick, and his performance reeled me back into the world of Bayview High hockey. Then I drew upon my journalism background to learn about junior hockey, NCAA scholarships, and letters of intent. After some Internet research, I crafted a list of questions. Now I just needed someone to give me the answers. I contacted the organization College Hockey Inc., and they were kind enough to grant me a telephone interview. What an amazing resource for players and their families. I'm incredibly grateful for the information they provided, which helped me to fix the holes in my storyline.

For the last several years, I've worked as a freelance book editor and helped more than a hundred writers to develop their manuscripts. I'm known for writing friendly but honest ten-page letters, outlining my feedback. I pretended that *Offsides* had been written by a client, which gave me enough distance to view it objectively. Or in this case, rip it to shreds. After all, it had been written by a teenager who hadn't mastered her writing skills yet, and the original draft hadn't gone through professional editing like *Face-Off* did.

Once I got going, writing in the voices of the McKendrick boys felt totally natural to me. The twenty-five year wall disappeared and it was as if no time had passed. Over the next six months, I rewrote every single word. I'm grateful to my teenage self though, as she provided the basic outline. My adult self fleshed it out and improved the writing. I have to admit, it was fun giving the boys cell phones and showing them texting and on social media. I left the time-frame ambiguous in the *Face-Off* second edition, but since I had to rework *Offsides* anyway, it made sense to bring it up to date.

If I'd written *Face-Off* today, I would have done a few things differently. I would've explained how the boys got into hockey, given more spunk to female characters, and made the father more three-dimensional. I was excited to address those areas in *Offsides*. I always knew there was more to the story. And in hindsight, I can see that if the book was published in the 1990s, it wouldn't have been as strong. This particular story works a lot better in the present.

It was also interesting as my original "outline" was penned by a teenager, but when I was rewriting it, I had a parent's perspective. Part of *Face-Off*'s charm is that it was written by a teen for teens. With *Offsides*, it was neat to have my teenage self collaborate with my adult self and to blend both perspectives.

I'd like to thank everyone who helped me with *Offsides*:

Thank you to College Hockey Inc. for demystifying the recruiting process; to hockey player Ryan Compton for the great suggestion of the bar down goal; to Ryan, Alex Smargon, and Colin Smargon for answering my questions about what it's like on the ice, the equipment they use, and how they practice at home; and to Jodi Compton Tillinghast, childhood friend and hockey mom, and to her husband Jim Tillinghast, for providing thorough responses to my questions, beta reading the book, and catching my mistakes. I never could have made the book sound as authentic without Jodi and her family.

Thank you to my oldest friend, Joanne Braley, the first person to read *Face-Off* (getting notebook pages in study hall) and the first to read the new *Offsides* (getting the manuscript as an email attachment—how times have changed!) for her encouragement and feedback; to my parent friends on Facebook for sharing the disastrous state of their sons' bedrooms and how they would handle the alcohol situation depicted in the book; to my own parents Fran and Larry Drumtra for their support of my writing career and for everything else over the years; to my husband Mark Juba for designing the amazing hockey covers, sharing his helpful suggestions, and for always being my best friend; and to my girls Lauren and Caitlin, for their patience and willingness to have a few too many pancake dinners when I was distracted by "my boys" T.J. and Brad.

I'd very much appreciate reviews on retail sites and any help spreading the word to families whose teens and tweens might welcome a hockey novel. Thank you for picking up a copy of *Offsides*, and I hope reading it brings as much enjoyment to your family as writing it did to me. Do you want a book three? If so, email me through my website www.stacyjuba.com and let me know!

Excerpt from Face-Off

Head-to-Head, Skate-to-Skate, It's Winner Takes All!
Rival twin brothers battle on and off the ice in this
hockey classic written when Stacy was just 16-years-old.
Discover why this compelling novel has appeared on so many
reading lists including Best Books for Young Teen Readers
Grades 7-10 and a list produced by the
Hockey Hall of Fame's Junior Education Program.

Brad's twin brother T.J. has gotten himself out of the
fancy prep school his father picked for him and into the public
high school Brad attends. Now T.J. is a shining new star on the
hockey team where Brad once held the spotlight. And he's
testing his popularity with Brad's friends, eyeing Brad's girl and
competing to be captain of the team. Meanwhile, the twins must
also cope with problems at home, including divorcing parents
and a troubled younger brother. The whole school is rooting for
a big double-strength win…not knowing that their twin hockey
stars are heating up the ice for a winner takes all face-off.

As Mrs. McKendrick and Chris followed Jory into the living room, Brad and T.J. stared at each other. Finally, T.J. said, "Look, you've been ticked at me since practice. You're mad that I got made cocaptain aren't you? Come on," T.J. said when Brad didn't respond. "I've got just as much right to it as you do."

Brad scoffed. "Hardly. I've been slaving on that team since I was a freshman."

"So? It's not like I've never played the game before."

"It doesn't matter. I've been playing for Bayview for three years and you haven't even played one game for them!"

"Look, it's not my fault that I got yanked out of Hayden! I didn't ask to go to Bayview. You think I wanted to leave all my friends and go to a new school? It's hard enough going there without you acting like such a jerk."

"You're the one who's acting like a jerk, T.J."

"You're just afraid that I'm going to do better than you, and you can't take it!"

"Are you kidding? You may be Dad's precious genius, but you're never going to be better than me at hockey. And if you think I'm playing on a line with you, you're crazy. So let's just see who Reynolds sends down a line, T.J.," Brad challenged his brother.

"Yeah, well have fun playing with McCann," T.J. snapped.

Brad shoved his brother into the refrigerator, and T.J. promptly pushed him back. They were grappling with each other when their father strode into the room and ripped them apart.

"What on earth is going on in here?" Mr. McKendrick demanded, his face red.

"Nothing," Brad said.

"Nothing?" Mr. McKendrick asked.

"Nothing other than the fact that T.J. is an obnoxious jerk."

"Hey, you're the one who's threatening to quit the line," T.J. said.

"I'm not threatening to quit the line. I'm threatening to get you kicked off it."

T.J.'s green eyes flashed. "Go to hell!"

"Look, I don't know what this is about," their father began, "but you two have an obligation to your teammates. You can't just go back on that because of personal differences."

"He started it," T.J. said.

"I don't care who started it. I just want it stopped."

Made in the USA
Middletown, DE
07 January 2019